Pollard shook his head. He adorned his face with his tightest smile. This was his signal that he was the adult who had the answers. "Christmas isn't about big things, Katie," said Pollard, chuckling. "It's about little things. Think little."

Matt thought of Liz and Jamie and Tack, for whom presents poured. He thought of Liz after she read his statement, "There is no Santa," regarding him with disturbing deepness, as if she saw down his mind. He thought of Jamie, paying no attention; and of Tack, smiling his eternal smile, as if life were good.

Matt was overwhelmed by the desire for Santa to be real. For Katie to have Santa.

"Think little," said Pollard again, tapping his pen.

Katie faded like an old sheet, as if she'd been washed too many times. Her hands came down slowly, and she sat on them, squishing out hope.

Caroline Cooney lives in Westbrook, Connecticut, and is the author of many novels for young readers.

What Child is This?

A Christmas story

Caroline B. Cooney

MACMILLAN
CHILDREN'S BOOKS

First published 1997 by Delacorte Press,
a division of Bantam Doubleday Dell Publishing Group Inc, USA

First published in the UK 1998 by Macmillan Children's Books
a division of Macmillan Publishers Limited
25 Eccleston Place, London SW1W 9NF
and Basingstoke

Associated companies throughout the world

ISBN 0 330 37053 7

1 3 5 7 9 8 6 4 2

A CIP catalogue record for this book is available from
the British Library.

Printed and bound in Great Britain by Mackays of Chatham plc, Kent

For all the churches whose organs
I have been privileged to play;
for all the carol services and Christmas Eves;
and with thanks to Sayre and Beverly

The silent stars go by

✦

It was Christmas Eve.

The pageant was full of crying babies and noisy sheep. The cherub choir sang, the candles were lit, the readings from Luke were said slowly, with love.

When the last verse of "Joy to the World" had been sung, a family walked home in snow. Last year, the snow had been as deep as Christmas carols, but this year, it was only a shimmer of white on the hard cold ground.

They collapsed on a soft plump sofa, snuggling tight up against each other, and it felt the way children feel under the covers at night, like time for a story. And so the child said, "Tell me about the first Christmas."

"You know all about the first Christmas," said her father. "You just saw the pageant. Mary and Joseph and the angel. The trek to Bethlehem. No room at the inn. Baby Jesus born in a stable."

"Not *his* first Christmas. *My* first Christmas."

That Christmas.

Last Christmas.

A December when the grown-ups left a lot to be desired. But oh!—the children desired so much.

When I was a seeker,
I sought both day and night

✦

Liz's parents were crazy for Christmas trees.

They never had just one tree, but filled the house with little backup, secondary-theme trees in each room. They might decorate a Christmas tree by color (silver, royal blue, sun gold), by creature (circus animals, Noah's Ark), by musical instruments (drum, trumpet, harp), or by heavenly delights (angels, stars, crescent moons).

Christmas was a major event for the Kitchell family.

Liz's father thought about Christmas as an innkeeper: in terms of houseguests. Dad wanted every relative, every old friend (for that matter, every stranger met on a cruise), to stay over. He thought in terms of food: the right drink for the right person, the largest turkey. Liz was pretty sure Dad never thought of another innkeeper, two thousand years ago, who hadn't had a place big enough.

The Kitchells' elegant Victorian house was definitely big enough. Size was important: at Christmas you wanted enough mantelpieces, enough stair landings and window ledges to strew your wreaths, your manger scenes, and your card collections. Age was important: their house was over a hundred years old, and everybody knew that people in the 1880s and the 1890s had done Christmas the best; in that century, they even used real candles on their trees.

But in real estate, it's location that matters, and the Kitchells had location: their fine lawn with its huge old maples and oaks joined the small park that surrounded a beautiful old Colonial church. The church was white clapboard, spare and lean, with tall sparkling windows and a high thin spire that narrowed like a gold exclamation point to God.

The Kitchells had never gone to church, nor considered it. They did, however, send Christmas cards with Vermont-style snow and steeples framed against a blue sky.

When Liz and her sister, Allison, were little, they'd made tree decorations in art: sheep from cotton balls, tree chains from colored paper, stars from felt and glitter. Their mother never put these up. They were imperfect, and Mrs. Kitchell believed in the perfection of a Christmas tree.

Liz and Allison's mother and father had bought a new Christmas tree holder to try out this year on the truly big tree in the formal living room. Usually you had to go to war with your tree, hefting it in the air, trying to lower it straight down into the holder, getting sap and needles in your eyes, while everybody else hollered that you had it crooked. With the new kind, you fastened the tree trunk in the cup while the tree was still lying down, and *then* you turned the tree upright, and it adjusted itself.

"One of the century's finer inventions," their father had said.

Liz sat in her English class and looked out the window, a trick everybody used when trying to think, as if the sky gave out ideas. It was snowing, the first snow of

3

the year. December snow was slow and toasty, like thick blankets.

Mrs. Wrenn had not bothered to prepare a lesson plan. This was a daily occurrence. She'd just fill the time with creative writing, which exempted her from effort. Mrs. Wrenn had long hard scarlet fingernails, which she spent much of the class period admiring. Now she clicked them on her desktop, in the rhythm of "Rudolph the Red-Nosed Reindeer."

"Today for our creative writing exercise," said Mrs. Wrenn, "your goal is one perfect paragraph." She liked paragraphs because there was less to correct. The class didn't mind. They liked paragraphs because there was less to write. "I'm setting the timer for ten minutes," she added.

Translation: the remaining thirty minutes of the period would be spent reading the stuff out loud.

At least it wasn't the VCR and a film clip.

Liz thought of yesterday's creative writing topic: "What was the most upsetting thing I witnessed this week?"

It was actually a pretty good assignment, and Liz had a pretty good first thought: *The most upsetting thing I witnessed this week was my parents watching television.*

Every night on the local newscast, needy people had their dreadful stories of loss and suffering and poverty taped and dissected. "At Christmas," said the reporter, "we must Remember the Neediest."

The camera work was brilliant. Slowly scanning a city block, it turned joyful Christmas into pain. You could tell that the hearts of the neediest were dried and split like old vinyl.

Liz had the loveliest home that money could create, and thirty seconds of the neediest made *her* feel homeless.

But Liz's parents were not interested in the neediest.

"Why should we have to look at that?" her father had said irritably. "Why can't they stick to reporting and stop laying guilt trips and demanding money?" He hit the Mute button.

The television continued to report, but without sound or effect.

"Let me show you what I bought today!" cried Liz's mother, who shopped at stores where the bags themselves were worth framing. She was a world-class, Olympic-level shopper. "The most beautiful beaded gold and green Christmas balls!" said her mother, taking them one by one from their wrapping of sparkly tissue. "They're from Spain."

"I love them!" her father said, holding each ball like a treasure. "Which tree shall we put them on?"

It was the first week in December, so the trees were up, but bare; still in the planning stage.

"Do you ever think about what Christmas means, Dad?" asked Liz. She kept her voice casual and quiet. "Do you ever think about that baby, and how—"

But in the Kitchell family, the word *baby* was not a good one.

"Liz," said her father, "I suppose we're Christian if we

5

fill out forms and don't want to check off *Islam,* but other than that, it's crap."

Liz hated that word. It was ugly and flat. She did not want anything in her life to be listed as *crap.* She sank back in her chair, not sure which baby she had been talking about, anyway.

Liz never saw a Christmas tree go up without wonderment. There was a strangeness to the whole thing that gave her prickles. Could there really be a God?

And when the star was carefully placed on top—naturally the Kitchells had a wide star selection; no tradition except the tradition of acquiring more—but when the new star was fastened to the top of the tree, brushing the ceiling, Liz had to close her eyes against a rush of thought.

I have to believe in stars and heavens and God, thought Liz, because if I don't—*What about the baby?*

The silent TV displayed an elderly woman living in fear and loneliness.

"I think these Spanish balls belong on the main tree in the living room," said her mother, juggling them gently.

So for the Most Upsetting Thing, Liz could have written that her family thought other people's suffering was a bore.

Liz didn't want to know that, never mind let her friends in on it. So she'd made a joke out of yesterday's assignment.

"The most upsetting thing I witnessed this week," wrote Liz, "was the dreaded moment when my mother

6

ran out of conditioner. It was a terrible thing to see—Mom draped over the sink, hair dripping wet, and no way to improve the texture."

She got an A: Liz always got an A. But she wanted one teacher, just once, to scrawl on the page: "What's with this flippant sarcasm? I'm sick of it. Write truth."

Liz was pretty confident that nobody ever considered writing the truth. The moment you set a pencil to a paper, or typed a word on a keyboard, the thought was outside your mind. In the brightness of day, or the sharpness of white paper, it got too intense. Better to keep truth to yourself, unvoiced and unwritten.

"Here is the topic for today," said Mrs. Wrenn. "What do you want for Christmas?"

I want to do something good, thought Liz, and she was hit by horror that, instead, she and her parents would do something bad.

"No! Wait! I've changed my mind!" said Mrs. Wrenn, who loved to do this; she felt she was being exciting and creative when she changed the assignment seconds after giving it. She smiled a sly greedy smile. "No, instead the question will be: How do you *get* what you want for Christmas?"

Liz felt clammy and heavy, like a sinking dory, full of murky salt water, and no oars.

Mrs. Wrenn liked teams in creative writing. "Tack Jamie Matt Liz," she said, as if Liz were a banana on a shopping list.

The high school had no desks, since no kid had ever used the desk storage area for anything but trouble. Long ago, tables for two had been substituted. This worked fine if you liked your table partner, but meant a really long year if you didn't.

Tack and Jamie shared a table, and had not moved, and were not going to move, so Matt and Liz dragged their chairs to Tack's table, where they crowded shoulder to shoulder.

Liz's friend Rachel winked at her, because it was a nice ratio, three boys to one girl, and Liz adored Tack Knight. She had looked up that word *adore*. The definition included "worship."

Liz was at that phase in a crush when it might cease to be a secret and instead, without permission, fill your mind and face and body, and even the classroom. What if Mrs. Wrenn saw her crush on Tack and commented cruelly? What if Tack saw . . . and didn't want it?

Through the depth and heat and nonsense of this crush (nonsense because Tack had never exhibited the slightest interest in her whatsoever), Liz could barely manage a normal conversation with Tack.

Tack's dad owned a restaurant where the Kitchells often dined, River Wind Inn, and it looked so cozy: your own beloved family running a business together, morning, noon, and night. At the restaurant, Tack was an adult, not a high-school kid. Liz was slightly uncomfortable watching him at the restaurant, as if he had grown up and she had failed to. Or as if his family worked and hers did not.

Oh! she hated being a traitor toward her parents.

But she wanted them to be different.

For Mom, there were no holidays, just decorations.

The last time Liz had ever tried to get Mom to think seriously had been Memorial Day, after the parade. The high-school band marched a full mile in their beautiful scarlet-and-white uniforms, and Liz played the clarinet, and they stopped at the old cemetery where the Civil War dead lay under the grass, and the American Legion had put flags beside each gray stone. Tack Knight played Taps on his trumpet, while Julie Millman, far away at the other side of the cemetery, played a lingering, desperately sad echo. They had studied the Civil War in preparation for this: talked about the death of more than six hundred thousand men, and the eighty-two teenagers in the marching band, at least, stared at the graves.

Liz's mother saw only photo opportunities. She darted here and there, while the rest of the parents had good manners, and stood still, and the men rested their caps against their hearts.

So Liz, who wanted to talk about death most of all, and babies second of all, let her mother go, and her mother went straight toward the next holiday, the Fourth of July, a terrific holiday, because of all those flags, the perfect graphic, with fine strong contrast of red, white, and blue.

Liz had dawdled, full of thought, and instead of getting to sit next to Tack, she ended up between Jamie and Matt.

Jamie was so bored by school that he in turn was totally boring to anybody else, and Matt was worthless. This meant nothing would distract her from Tack.

9

"Everybody ready?" said Mrs. Wrenn, as if she planned to name out loud anybody too dumb to be ready. "I'll start the timer."

I'm not ready, thought Liz. Christmas is coming, and I don't know why.

Bearing gifts, we traverse afar

✦

Tack flipped open his blue cloth binder, snapped the three metal rings apart, removed a piece of blank paper, and picked up his pencil. He was both relieved and sorry when Liz ended up between the other guys instead of next to him. Tack was slightly afraid of Liz. She felt too cool to him, as if she kept a lower body temperature than other people. Liz seemed to revise her sentences before she talked. Tack was more relaxed with people who just blurted stuff out, stupid or not, and you knew who they were.

Tack let his eyes drift equally over his three partners: Jamie, Liz, and Matt. At this distance, he could sort of admire Liz, instead of get confused by her.

Mrs. Wrenn loved trendy topics: sex, of course, and violence, and people's rights. But anything that mattered—generosity or kindness—and she was out of there. For Tack, this just meant she wasn't worth thinking about, so he didn't.

What do I want for Christmas? thought Tack. Easy. I want the best restaurant tree ever.

His grin spread across his face.

Tack had been teased all his life for that grin: he couldn't keep a blank face like the other guys. Whenever he was pleased with something, there was his face, letting the world know. Everybody else in class could be frown-

11

ing or complaining or even gagging over some maddening assignment, while Tack, whose mind was elsewhere, would be grinning like an idiot. In junior high, he'd adopted a posture of keeping his hand over his mouth. People figured he had braces to hide. But it was too much trouble, getting his hand up there in time, so Tack learned to live with it, this dumb grin that rode around like a horse on the loose.

Of course, he would never write about the restaurant trees, no matter how happy they made him. He'd never expose anything so precious to Mrs. Wrenn's skeptical eyes. Mrs. Wrenn never wanted her students to take anything—least of all religion—seriously. If a kid ever wrote something deep, or awed, or private, Mrs. Wrenn would read it aloud, mocking it. She would roll her eyes at the rest of the class. She had very long thin fingers and matching long scarlet nails, and she would rest this rather eerie hand on her victim's shoulder and make some slick comment, egging the class to laugh at the kid too.

It did not surprise Tack that Mrs. Wrenn would pick a selfish topic: How do you get what you want?

But as he planned the paragraph—because he'd be the first to write—he was surprised to realize that that defined December for him: how to be sure kids got what they wanted for Christmas.

I could tell the truth, he thought, I could write: *What this classroom really needs is a restaurant tree.*

However, Tack liked a good grade. One of his skills was to psych out his teachers, and give them what they wanted, and get an A. He wrote:

12

> There are two guys involved in
> Christmas. God and Santa.

Mrs. Wrenn would like that: making God no more than a fat guy in a mall wearing red velour.

> God brings stuff like peace in your heart.
> You cannot set out milk and cookies for God
> and get a leather jacket or CDs in return.
> Therefore at Christmas, aim for Santa.

Tack reread this, liked it, and handed the page to Jamie. Jamie was paying no attention and had to be kicked. Liz had read it upside down and was ready to add to it. Matt of course was sitting motionless with that duct-tape look of his: I'm taped, you're taped, we're all taped shut. With Matt you had no access. Matt had the usual openings—ears, mouth—but he didn't use them.

From the rich to the poor they are mostly unkind

✦

Matt Morden was a person of rage.

He felt that he had studied himself in geology. He was molten lava, his core was fury. The thing was to keep that heat down, to put asphalt or grass over it.

Sometimes he wondered about the core of other people: people who had everything, like Tack and Liz.

Were their cores like steel, gleaming and unbending? Like ice cream, melted and soft?

Based on what Tack had written for the Christmas paragraph, Tack's core was air.

Matt was last in the four-person writing row. When his turn came, two good students (Tack and Liz) and one person you couldn't even call a student, because he so completely didn't care what was going on (Jamie), would turn to look at Matt, and they would weigh his potential. Matt had no potential in English, and they knew it.

Matt admired Tack for starting. Tack was always willing to start, whereas Matt had to watch ten examples, or wait a year, before he could do something the first time. It was Matt's definition of manhood: that you started off without looking around.

Whenever Matt wrote something, Mrs. Wrenn would flap it around, making little paper smacking noises. "Open up, Matthew, open up!" she would cry.

Like Matt would ever open up to somebody with the personality of her own fingernails.

Aim for Santa, he thought, staring at Tack's sentence. It's the other way around, Tack. Christmas has to aim for you.

Tack had slouched back in his hard plastic chair, eyelids lowered, jaw skewed sideways. He was rereading his own sentences with a you'll-never-match-this look of superiority. Matt decided that what Tack really needed for Christmas was a good slug in that same jaw.

But then Tack grinned at him. It was a whole-face grin, and it said: Hey, Matt, I'm with you, I can't stand Mrs. Wrenn either.

Matt had the same name as half the boys in school, but Tack, short for Thomas Knight, initials TK, therefore Tack, was a one and only. Tack had the kind of face to which people always—*always;* Matt watched it every night at the restaurant, where he washed dishes—returned the expression. When Tack laughed, the patrons laughed. When Tack grinned, the patrons grinned. What an infectious smile! people would say, smiling.

Matt did not have smiles.

His facial expressions had been transferred to his gut. Instead of frowns, he got cramps. The muscles around his ribs would seize up and bind his lungs. Sometimes in the shower, he actually checked himself for bruises, because by the end of the day, his sides ached from holding in his rage.

Matt rarely exchanged glances with anybody. It didn't pay. He didn't understand what they wanted, and even though this was the kind of connection Pollard (and every other social worker he'd ever endured) wanted him to make, Matt found all connection false.

Except the Rowens.

He was almost fond of Mr. and Mrs. Rowen. It softened him, and in a strange new way, he didn't ache in the gut when he thought of Mr. and Mrs. Rowen.

Matt was not in the habit of talking to people whose house he would leave in a month or two. So last July when Pollard had brought Matt to the Rowens, Matt had nothing to say. He knew good manners required him to respond when spoken to, but he was not within the reach of manners. He had to spend the summer peeling his mother out of his mind. The Rowens' house was as good or as bad a place as any; he didn't care.

He did not refer to the Rowens as foster parents or foster family, because parents kept you, and families were related to you. The Rowens were just people, and he was just passing through.

There was one surprise at the Rowens': Mrs. Rowen was an excellent cook. She would actually bake a row of pies or sheet after sheet of cookies. She was pretty good at silence herself and would spoon up a big hunk of raw cookie dough, studded with chocolate chips, and hand it over to Matt without saying a word. He loved cookie dough. If she made a cake, she'd hand him the bowl and a rubber spatula so that he could finish the sweet thick batter. Sometimes she made this apple thing, buttery layers and sweetness and crunch that made him hang out in the kitchen, waiting.

Then, in September, school started. It was a new

school; Matt was always having to be a new kid at a new school; and in spite of all he had been through with his mother—the streets, the fear, the cops—Matt was still afraid of a simple thing like the first day of school.

Matt had no expectations of school. The Rowens did.

Every night, during supper, Mr. or Mrs. Rowen would turn to him. "What'd you do in school today, Matt?"

He would shrug.

They'd stare back, not blinking, not moving, not reaching for the television remote. Just patiently waiting for an answer.

Matt could wait longer than any ten adults, so he remained silent. He did not want to discuss school, which was mostly full of things he did not have, like friends.

But Mrs. Rowen, come September, changed the rules. Over raw dough, she allowed silence. At the dinner table, to get dessert on a plate, dessert baked and hot from the oven, Matt had to speak.

If Matt didn't speak to get his dessert, Mrs. Rowen would calmly wrap the pies or cupcakes in freezer paper, and mark them slowly, with a black pen, and stack them in the freezer.

Matt felt like a puppy being paper-trained ("Good boy, here's a biscuit"). But he loved her desserts. Sometimes it was what kept him going through the school morning—knowing that she had packed a slice of pie in his lunch bag; and sometimes it kept him going through the afternoon—knowing that in a few hours, he could sit silently in her kitchen, amid the safety and joy of food.

Like a puppy, Matt obeyed the rules. Sort of. He

would use a single word to get his dog biscuit. "What did you do today?" they would ask. "Nothing," he would say. Or, "School."

No dessert would be handed over.

Mr. Rowen would go: "And?"

Matt would stare at him, blank. Matt was good at blank. In his official file, they wrote "not bright," and although Matt knew he was smart, he agreed he was not bright. His light was dim, his heart closed.

Verbally, Mr. Rowen would trudge through the class day. "First period?" he'd demand.

"Algebra."

"And?"

"Seventy-seven."

"Not good enough. How come you didn't do better?"

Nobody had ever asked Matt why he didn't do better. Foster children were expected to do badly, because of their failed self-esteem and all. "Nuts," said Mr. Rowen. "You're smart. Get an A."

Matt got an A.

When he came home from school, he set that math paper on the kitchen counter. Naturally, he didn't say anything. Mrs. Rowen didn't notice it. She was busy kneading bread. Matt asked if he could try. After he washed his hands, she said. Matt thought she would pick up his math test while he kneaded, but she didn't.

For the rest of the afternoon, Matt lay on his back on his bed, and his ribs and his shoulders hurt.

When Matt was called for dinner, the counter had been scrubbed and the test was gone.

They had thrown it out.

He stared around, disoriented by the loss of his first and only A. He had actually studied to get that A. It was the first time Matt really understood what *studying* meant. He had actually enjoyed taking his mind in his hands and attaching it firmly to the page.

They had thrown his A out.

He did not see how he could eat. The muscles in his gut were strangling him.

Then he saw, taped to the white refrigerator, not just his A, but his A in a frame: they had taped a piece of bright red construction paper up first, and then taped the math test on top of it. Matt remembered this from elementary school: how other kids, kids with families, would describe this: "My mom put it on the refrigerator," they would say.

"Nice," said Mrs. Rowen, patting the A. She smiled. "You can have dessert first, if you want."

"Get more A's, Matt," said Mr. Rowen, and then he picked up the remote and turned to the television.

So Matt did. Every A got a frame on the refrigerator. Mrs. Rowen was working her way down a stack of construction paper, and by now the red backing had been used up, and they were in orange, soon to reach lime green, and Matt detested both orange and green, but he did not want to say so; he did not want to whine, "Let's go to the store and buy just red paper."

In algebra, along with A's, he got something he had never had before: understanding. *He understood this subject.*

And he got something else he'd never had: a teacher interested in him. Thinking became fun. He rarely spoke in Mrs. Simmetti's class, but the numbers talked for him: he could use them; they did not fail him the way speech did. Mrs. Simmetti began to speak of Matt's joining the math team, of which Tack was captain. The team went in a van, like a sports team, from school to school, competing in real events.

"Me?" asked Matt.

"You're not ready yet," Mrs. Simmetti told him, "but I want you to get practice. By January you'll be at competition level, and you need to be relaxed and comfortable for your first meet."

Matt had never been relaxed and comfortable for anything. He did not take her up on her invitation. He thought about being on a team with Tack, rather than being a dishwasher for Tack, but he could not see himself on this team. He didn't go. Tack mentioned it a few times at the restaurant, and Matt was startled and even a little bit proud that Mrs. Simmetti had told the math team she was thinking about him, but he said nothing to Tack, and he didn't go to a practice.

And then Katie arrived.

The Rowens took Katie under pressure. "She's too little for us," said Mrs. Rowen.

"We usually just take boys," said Mr. Rowen.

"We're desperate," said Pollard. "Poor little Katie," cried Pollard. "Just for a few weeks, then we'll place her somewhere else."

Matt was the right age for the Rowens, who were no longer young and who were tired of being foster parents. Matt could do everything for himself: studying, laundry, getting to and from school, keeping a job. The Rowens just had to provide a roof, a bed, hot meals, and a few minutes of talk.

Katie was the wrong age. She wanted laps and hugs; she wanted somebody to color with her, and watch cartoons with her, and argue over snacks with her. She wanted to be read to, and talked to, and taken places.

The Rowens had enough energy for Matt. They did not have enough for Katie and Matt.

A few weeks became a month, and one month was close to two. And Pollard had nowhere to put Katie. And the Rowens were fading.

"How's your little sister doing?" Pollard liked to say when he came to the house to check on them.

Matt was not Katie's brother. He refused to pretend he was. We're passing through. She's a stranger and I'm a stranger and the Rowens are strangers. I am not her brother!

Matt was so angry with Katie for wrecking his life with the Rowens. He tried not to be. This was not her fault, any more than his life was his fault. But he was angry anyway. It was a true fault, like the San Andreas Fault in California. Matt had a fault of the soul.

If Mr. and Mrs. Rowen called Pollard and said they couldn't handle two kids anymore—and Katie and Matt had to go—he, at least, was finished.

Even though none of the house changes had been his fault, the foster-care system kept track of the number of families you were placed with. It was a road that came to an end.

If you didn't work out living with some generous decent family, and then didn't work out again, and then

21

still didn't work out—well, after six or seven tries, you got sent to Cambridge.

Cambridge was the Children's Home.

Not an orphanage. Few kids were orphans. Cambridge was a place to stack kids when regular parents in regular foster homes could not control them.

Cambridge was the Bad Kid Corral.

Cambridge had the high chain-link fence, and the gate, and the motion sensors. Cambridge had dormitories: four kids to a room. It had counselors and social workers . . . and guards.

It wasn't Matt's fault.

Like last year, when his mother suddenly reappeared and wanted him back.

Matt always fell for this, because he wanted nothing more than his mother. When they asked him if he wanted to go, he said yes, because he did, even though he knew, and they knew, and certainly his mother knew, that it was not going to work, because she was off drugs this afternoon, but she'd be on again by next week.

So Matt left the foster home, and he and his mother tried once again to be a family, and this time Matt lasted three months with her, three months from hell, and yet he loved her, and covered for her, and faked it for them both. And when she was back in jail, and when they sent Matt back into the foster-care system, of course the family he'd been with had another kid now and didn't have room for Matt, and so he was sent to another house, and he could not blame his mother; he could not stand blaming his mother; and he could not blame himself, because he could never figure out what he would have done differently.

He did not know if the day would come when he could ignore his mother.

He thought that when he finally grew up, and was old enough, he would join the army. Maybe the air force, because he loved to look up and see jet trails in the sky. It shook his heart to think of people going those great distances, to worlds he had never seen; and he thought if the air force stationed him two thousand miles away, he would be safe.

He loved to look at generals on television: General Powell, General Shalikashvili. They looked so sturdy inside their uniforms, so sure of things.

Matt believed that a uniform would button him into another personality; he could shine himself, salute himself, shave himself, into another life.

He believed this like religion. If he could hang on long enough, if he could reach eighteen, he could make it to the army, or the air force, and there would be his safety.

If he were put in Cambridge, it would count as reform school. It would be on record that he was unmanageable, was bad. And what air force would take him then? What army?

How do I get what I want for Christmas? thought Matt, staring at Tack's large, handsome handwriting. If only I knew.

"Come, come, come!" said Mrs. Wrenn, drumming her fingernails on the blackboard. "You've spent two important minutes!"

23

Matt especially loathed Mrs. Wrenn when she talked to them as if to a kindergarten class. Perhaps he would give her finger paints for Christmas. Or Pampers, depending on how infantile she was being.

Jamie twirled Tack's pencil.

Jamie was an okay person who had no interest in school and just sat through it. He was a body in a chair. Matt envied him, because Matt could not withdraw quite that completely. Jamie wrote:

> Santa does know if you've been naughty
> or nice, but Christmas is not school. There
> won't be a quiz. Nobody fails the grade.

Matt felt a chill as great as January in his bones. Christmas as school. A grade you could fail.

And Matt, yes, had failed every year. An F in Christmas.

Christmas took a long time coming. It gathered speed, and size, and volume. It gathered songs and snow and gift wrap and hope, until it was this enormous avalanche, and Matt would think . . . Maybe if I stand in its path . . . maybe . . . maybe this year . . .

But no. Never this year, nor last year, and not next year either.

For Matt, every December phrase was a phrase gone wrong. When the high school had an open house, it seemed a mockery. How many houses were really open? How many really let you in? How many kids had a roof but not a home? Parents, but not love? Keys to the door, but nobody glad to see them walk in?

Even if you don't have a single check in your Nice column, and all year you've been nothing but Naughty, Santa will still pour presents under the tree.

Matt wanted to know just who this Santa was who poured presents under trees.

All our costliest treasures bring

·✦·

It was certainly true for Liz. The Kitchells bought tons of gifts for one another, and the wrapping of these gifts was a very satisfying December activity. Sometimes there were so many presents that they spread out from under the tree, and across the room, and up onto the coffee table.

This year not only were her sister, Allison, and Allison's husband, Daniel, coming for Christmas, but also elderly cousins they hadn't seen in ages, plus Mom's college roommate and her husband and a couple on some committee with Dad. It would be a full house.

Last night, during the Neediest, her mother had said, "Charlie! I have the most wonderful idea! What do you think of this! Maybe I'll start a Christmas shop! I'd be open from July through December twenty-fourth. Wouldn't it be fun?"

Her parents discussed how much money this would take, and whether the city was the right place for it, or should they pick a cute little Early American shopping mall, with dark red shingles and a cupola with a rooster on top.

It made Liz crazy that her parents could talk continually about Christmas—shop, decorate, triple their trees—and never, not once, ever, be willing to talk about the baby.

Liz wanted to write: *I don't know how to get what I want. When Death has taken what you want, how do you get it back? How do you get anything back—happiness or goodness or joy? Where do you apply? Who do you write the letter to?*

It was her turn. She must be shallow and casual and touch no truth. She wrote:

> The key to getting more presents on
> Christmas is to have more chimneys.
> Be sure to purchase a charming
> old house with four fireplaces.
> Santa will deliver four times as many gifts.

Liz was rewarded with a grin from Tack. He didn't have dimples, but long grin lines on the sides of his face, deep as an old man's, as if he'd been grinning for decades. When he stopped grinning, the lines went away and he looked very young. Liz found this incredibly appealing. She wanted to trace the grin lines with her fingertips, or kiss them, and so she had to look away and pretend she did not even know who Tack was or whether he had a face at all.

Jamie actually raised his eyebrows and nodded to show his approval of her sentences. High attention.

Matt, of course, being a sociopath with no normal emotions or reactions, just sat there.

Actually, the only private conversation Tack and Liz had ever had was about Matt. "My father says," said Tack—Liz loved how Tack was always quoting his father—"My father says Matt is damaged goods. He says you have a life like Matt's and you have too many scars to climb out."

Tack's father had hired Matt as a busboy. Matt had been working last time the Kitchells ate at River Wind Inn—silent and dull, clearing tables, not acknowledging that he knew Liz.

"Maybe he'll rescue himself," Liz had said, and heard the cruel shape of her sentence: it was Matt's responsibility to do any rescue; it wasn't her responsibility, or the school's, or the world's.

Tack shook his head. "My father says it's too late for rescue. Matt is doomed."

Liz had been horrified.

"I know," said Tack, reading her expression. "I· feel that way too. It should never be too late."

Now, in English, Liz thought of Allison's baby, for whom it was too late; of Allison, for whom it might also be too late.

Maybe Liz's mother was right. Stay with pretty decorations. Forget the soul.

Then Tack smiled again, grin lines just for her.

Liz decided that what she really wanted for Christmas was Tack.

Many there be that stand outside

✦

"O-kay, Matt!" said Liz, smacking the paper and pencil down in front of Matt. She gave him a bright-eyed *on your mark, get set, go!* look.

Matt struggled to come up with anything at all to write about Christmas.

Every year, against his will, as Christmas approached, Matt found himself hoping.

Hope would begin a little after Thanksgiving, and it would get large and starry, and he would find himself lying awake at night, as if Hope kept his eyes from closing.

He did not know what he hoped for.

But sometimes it was so intense he had trouble breathing, and then he had to steady himself against Christmas.

Matt finished up the paragraph. As usual, he did not have much to say. As usual, he could not make anything up. For Matt, there was silence or there was truth. He could not get in between, like other people. He wrote:

> There's only one problem.
> There is no Santa.

What child is this?

·✦·

On that same Thursday, in an elementary school a mile and a quarter away, the third grade had a spelling test.

Mrs. Halsey had given them a list of December words: *snow, candle, gift, tree, menorah, winter, ribbon, reindeer, cold, holly, light.*

There were some difficult words in that list.

Mrs. Halsey walked quietly among the desks while the children struggled. She positioned herself between Katie and Katie's view of Emily's paper. Emily hardly ever missed a spelling word. Katie, whose school background was checkered, to say the least, would panic during a test and grip her pencil so tightly she tore the paper. Katie was always tempted to squint and see how Emily was spelling the word.

Katie hungered and thirsted to be touched.

Back when Mrs. Halsey began teaching, twenty years ago, she'd been a hugger and a kisser, constantly putting her hand on the top of a child's head, or in the center of a child's back, or resting it on a shoulder. Nothing gave a scared little kid courage more quickly than a touch.

But you had to be so careful now: a simple hug, an easy warm way to show a little kid you liked her, could be a true danger. You could find yourself accused of some terrible crime when all you wanted to say was, Katie, I like you the way you are, it's only spelling, relax and it will work for you.

It was a loss to teaching, that you could not show a little girl some affection.

Besides, nothing could be spontaneous now; it must be planned and divided equally. If you hugged one child, you had to hug the other twenty-six, and there was not time.

Mrs. Halsey loved December. She loved art and making things for display. She loved colored paper and metallic tape and little bottles of glitter. This year she'd brought her angel collection into school and set it out on the wide counter that ran the length of the window wall. Papier-mâché angels and brass angels and painted wooden angels. Baby angels, Renaissance angels, felt angels. Angels with long flying gold hair and angels made of spun glass.

More than any of the other children, Katie was drawn to the angels. She touched them very gently, holding her breath, as if it were an honor.

Sometimes Mrs. Halsey thought of letting Katie take whatever angel she wanted. After all, there were over a hundred angels now. But if Mrs. Halsey gave one child an angel, she'd have to give the rest an angel, and there'd be no end to it.

Last week they'd had Lunchtime Open House in Third Grade, and the parents made an effort and got there. Every child except Katie had one parent, or two, and several had three or four, plus grandparents. Katie sat alone at her desk, holding her folder of papers that no parent was going to look at, and Mrs. Halsey kept meaning to go over and console Katie, but there were so many parents to talk to, and she kept forgetting and then open house was over.

Mrs. Halsey hated to think about Katie's Christmas. I must call the social worker, she said to herself. I must be sure somebody does something for this child. There must be an agency, or a group, that would help.

"Candle," she said carefully, enunciating the spelling word so that everybody could hear the letters. It was a hard word. All around the class, anxious children wrote *candul, candole, cantuld.*

Katie did the oddest thing. She drew a candle instead, and it was lovely, with a curling flame, and shiver of wax on the side, and Emily looked over and said, "Oooh, Katie, how pretty! Mrs. Halsey, give her an A for *candle.*"

"I'm afraid this isn't art," said Mrs. Halsey. "Katie, you must remember to study your words at home."

For all weary children, Mary must weep

✦

In Katie's classroom were several children who did not speak English. She loved to hear them after school, speaking to their brothers and sisters in their own language. It was nice to know there were other people besides Katie who had no idea what was going on. But inside their own words—deep inside their own families—they knew.

If I had a family, Katie thought, I would know. What would I know?

She wasn't sure. But it would be something larger and finer than what she knew now, like a whole foreign language.

A family, thought Katie.

A home.

A house you come back to every day. All the time. For good.

Katie imagined the hallway of that house. How it would have a bench, and a coat closet, and be filled with mittens and basketballs and bookbags and snow boots and mail; filled with keys and scarves and a newspaper and coats sagging off their hangers.

There would be carpet everywhere, so you could go barefoot and your feet wouldn't get cold.

There would be a puppy; it would be golden and lick

your face. Its tail would wag so hard you had to get out of the way.

The television would be on, but when you came in, they'd turn it down, so they could talk to you. You'd sit on their laps, and their hugs would last and last.

Not hugs like social workers gave: quick as grades.

Hugs like mothers gave: wrapping-you-up hugs.

Hugs like fathers gave: hoisting-you-into-the-air and tossing-you-around hugs.

That Thursday after school, Emily waved and called, "Bye, Katie!"

Katie was immeasurably pleased. "Bye, Emily," she said, proud of her two words.

Emily got into a van, and Katie could see Emily's mother at the wheel, and Emily's little sister in a car seat in the back, and she saw Emily hand her spelling paper to her mother first, before they even drove away, and she imagined what it would be like to hand your spelling paper to your mother before you even drove away.

Once when Katie got eight out of ten right on an arithmetic test, Mrs. Rowen gave her a bear hug. Katie was sure that was what a bear hug was: that squashed feeling in your chest from somebody else's arms.

She thought of that hug all the time. She couldn't get over the heat in Mrs. Rowen's arms. How for that brief moment, warmth was hers.

But mostly, at the Rowens', only Matt could have a slot. Mr. and Mrs. Rowen were mostly too tired. Katie wanted so badly to sit in their laps, feel their arms around her, know that they would have come to the open house if they could.

She got on the bus. She was not afraid of the big kids, because Katie was acquainted with real danger, and this pleasant neighborhood had little of that. But she was afraid of sitting alone. There was something terrible and permanent about sitting alone on the school bus, even though the ride lasted only ten minutes.

She sat alone, thinking about Christmas. Christmas was such a calendar holiday. There was such shape to it: the forward march, the excitement, the music and color of it. And then every year it ended as if it had never been. January stepped up, and Christmas was gone.

For some reason, instead of getting excited about Christmas, the Rowens were kind of mad. As if it had no right to come. Katie tried to figure out where she stood in this; how to get out of the way of it; how to be still and quiet, so that the Rowens would not call Pollard to take Katie away.

Being a foster kid was like living in a blender. Life was always flinging you against sharp blades.

But amazingly, as Christmas approached, Matt was suddenly willing to help Katie with spelling and arithmetic. Matt was silent but mean; mean from years of no family . . . and Matt helped her.

She wondered if he would let her walk with him part of the way to the restaurant when he went to work tonight. Sometimes he did, and sometimes he would let her stop and talk about the pretty decorations people had. Once, he had held her hand.

The hopes and fears of all the years

⁺∗⁺

Matt got off the school bus and headed home.

Thursdays he worked at the restaurant from six to ten. That gave him a couple of hours to do schoolwork and relax before he headed to River Wind Inn. It was a nice walk in any weather. By now he knew every house he would pass, and the cars in their driveways, and the dogs in their yards. It made him comfortable to recognize places, to know that he was not a stranger here.

The snow had just finished falling. His were the very first steps. He liked the crunch of his sneaker treads, the little squeak that made a record of his passing. He had no boots, and sometimes he thought about boots; about what it would be like to walk in snow and not get wet socks.

Matt turned the corner to the street on which the Rowens lived. People here liked their Christmas celebration outside. They had decorations in their doorways, on their roofs, over their shrubs, in their gardens. Twig reindeer stood in front of a small green ranch house. A fat pine tree next to the sidewalk was heavily draped in blinking red, green, and yellow, like a traffic light factory. Seven dwarfs cut from plywood were carrying Christmas presents up a roof.

Matt actually felt his face relax in the direction that a

smile might take. Christmas truly was a mystery. He had no idea what people were trying to do here.

When he touched the fat tree, a crisp cinnamon scent filled his hand like a package, and the smile actually moved out on his face, almost there; almost real.

He glanced toward home. The word settled in his mind.

Home.

For the first time in years, he was calling a building with bedrooms a home.

Pollard's car was parked in the driveway.

Thursday?

Pollard came on Monday, if he came at all.

For a minute Matt could not walk, could not lift the bottoms of his feet, could not bend his legs at the knee.

Pollard was standing right in the Rowens' doorway, as if it were his house. As if he owned something there. But of course, he did. He owned Matt and Katie.

It was Matt's fault. It was the leaves. He hadn't raked.

The yard had been deep with the last maple leaves, and when he had heard the forecast for snow, Mr. Rowen had told Matt to finish the raking, and Matt had not. He was sick of leaves.

That's why Pollard was here. The Rowens were keeping this kid Matt out of the goodness of their hearts, and the kid couldn't even bother to clean up the yard in return. Send him to Cambridge.

Matt bought a minute by kneeling to retie his sneaker laces. The snow was still crisp and beautiful.

In the doorway, Pollard lifted his palm for Matt to

high-five, but Matt ignored it. It was all he could do not to throw Pollard into the bushes or stab him with an icicle. He and his caseworker were not buddies. There was nothing between them but business.

Matt moved past Pollard into the house.

Matt could smell the coffee Mrs. Rowen left on all day, while it got older and stronger. She took in typing, sitting for hours in front of her computer, typing, typing, typing, and sometimes she was still at it long into the night, her keyboard clicking as fast as the pulse of a hummingbird. Matt had never heard her complain. The computer array filled the little dining room, so they always ate in the kitchen, and her only breaks from work were baking breaks: she loved to mix and stir and whip and taste.

He had never touched her. He had never hugged her.

It was too late.

Mrs. Rowen waved at him from her keyboard. Mr. Rowen would not be home for two hours. By then, whatever had been decided would have come to pass, and Matt would be at the restaurant, scalding his hands for the sake of other people's dirty dishes.

Matt went into the living room. Puffy old chairs had faded old blankets tucked in around the cushions, because the stuffing was coming out. Throw rugs on the gnarly carpet had curled up, exposing stains. People with beautiful houses and extra bedrooms and baths did not have foster children. Only people with not enough bedrooms had foster children. This was a mysterious fact that Matt always wanted to point out to people like Liz and Jamie and Tack with their huge houses and their Santas who poured.

Mrs. Rowen had Christmas CDs playing. She loved carols. She loved all those songs about a child born in joy.

Matt did not know what he thought of Christmas carols. Everyplace but music, children were squandered like gambling bets.

He could not look at Katie.

He thought of the math team he had not joined. He was out of time now. He had taken too long to look around, and the traffic pattern had changed and he could never cross that street. Even if they found another foster home for him and Cambridge was postponed, he wouldn't end up in the same high school; that never happened.

He thought of calling Mr. Knight and asking for help.

He could not think about Tack and Tack's father at the same time. He knew, without letting himself dwell on it, that seeing this perfect father and son together evening after evening was too much for him. If he let himself imagine having a father in the way that Tack had a father, he felt as if he were being chopped by one of the huge professional knives the chefs used. So he could not think about father and son.

But separately—as a man who owned a restaurant and paid Matt a salary—Matt could think of Mr. Knight.

Mr. Knight seemed exactly correct to Matt, in a way that no other grown-up ever had. It was not just that he looked right—a father-looking kind of guy—and not just that he acted right—a fair kind of guy—but also that he seemed to know things. Important things. Things beyond where Matt was, beyond worry and anger; out there someplace else, where things worked out.

But even if Matt could imagine asking for help, he could not imagine help. Mr. Knight would be willing to do a little, but Matt could not ask him to do a lot, like find Matt a real home. Nobody was ever willing to do a lot.

Matt found that he could not swallow. His mouth was filling up. He massaged his throat, trying to find the stuck swallow.

He forced himself to look at Katie.

She was little enough that pleasing the social worker still mattered. For Pollard she had stuck on a smile, in a desperate, last-ditch effort to stay here. Her smile was false and stretched, like a puppy at the pound knowing this was the last chance. She knew as well as Matt that Mondays were social worker days; a Thursday visit could only be bad.

Katie's hair was the exact same color as Liz's, a deep rich brown, as if there were red underneath. Liz's hair hung in shiny curves, like the fender of a sports car. Every morning Mrs. Rowen brushed Katie's hair back tightly in a ponytail, warning Katie to keep it neat. To divide herself from Pollard, Katie had pulled her ponytail around to the front and was brushing her lips with it.

Matt's hand moved without his permission. It was unexpected, because Matt had total control over his exterior. But the hand went of its own choice to Katie and rested on her thin shoulder. He didn't do anything, didn't pat or squeeze.

Katie looked up, and into his eyes, a trespass Matt did not usually permit. Her awful pinched smile disappeared, and she just looked sad. That was better.

Why would I think sadness is better than a fake smile? he thought, and fleetingly he thought that if Mrs. Wrenn had been a different person, he could have written down a sentence like that.

Instead of leaning against the wall, his usual choice (sitting in Pollard's presence made Matt feel even more powerless), Matt sat next to Katie on the lumpy couch. They did not touch, but it made a tiny team out of them, his first attempt at such a thing.

Foster children could pack quickly. Every move Matt had ever made took only minutes, whereas when real people moved, they spent weeks getting ready, filling huge vans and leaving a trail of cardboard cartons across an entire yard.

One suitcase, one box, one duffel bag, one bookbag, and Matt would be done.

Even less for Katie.

41

All the bells on earth shall ring

※

But Pollard had come about Christmas. From his ratty old briefcase, Pollard took a stack of white paper bells.

The paper was thick and rich. Each bell had a slender gold cord for hanging on a tree. Pollard took two bells from the top of the stack. On one, he wrote in cramped square printing MATT. On the other, he wrote KATIE. On the back, very small, he wrote numbers: codes followed foster children everywhere they went.

"These bells," said Pollard, "get hung on Christmas trees in restaurants." Pollard not only stretched his face into a false smile, but his voice into fake cheer. "Including River Wind Inn, Matt, where you work."

Matt had no response.

"I write down your first name, and your age, and the Christmas present you want. Then if we're lucky, somebody eating out at that restaurant will see your Christmas wish and decide to get you the present." Pollard beamed his yellow nicotine-stained smile. "We can't promise anything. I don't want you to have false hopes. But mostly you get your wish. On Christmas morning, you'll probably have a present from a kind stranger under the tree."

No promises.

If we're lucky.

False hopes.

A present (that's singular; that's one) *under the tree.*

Matt could not stand the thought that a bell with his name on it would hang on the sweet-smelling tree that had just gone up in the hall between the bar and the dining room at River Wind Inn. He could not stand it that the chef, the waiters, the prep cook, the banquet manager all would see his bell and read what he was begging for, read about what he would not get if they chose not to be kind and generous to a foster kid. He would hate them if they were kind and generous, and he would hate them if they were not.

He hated Mr. Knight for having a restaurant tree, and he hated the world for not letting him, Matt, and her, Katie, be like Tack and Jamie and Liz and believe in Santa.

Matt gathered up the pieces of himself, trying to leave the rage alone, until he could leave for work. "I'm too old. Do one for Katie."

Matt earned pretty good money at River Wind Inn. He could have bought Katie some of the stuff she wanted so much: a Barbie, a teddy bear backpack, Disney stuff. He was suddenly a little shocked that it had never crossed his mind to spend anything on Katie.

"How about clothes, Matt? You want Levi 501's?" Pollard's voice dropped, getting sympathetic and kind. "I'll see that your bell is hung someplace else."

Matt hated it that Pollard could understand him. Matt wanted to be grown up, be on his own, have his own life. He wanted nobody. He did not want to be threatened with things like Christmas and luck.

"Whatever," said Matt. This was a useful word. It never failed to annoy grown-ups. Adults couldn't stand it when you were indifferent to their good works.

That's what I'll be at River Wind, he told himself. Indifferent. It works. Forget Tack and his father. Forget math team. Just wait, eventually it'll be over, don't connect.

"Action figures, Matt," Pollard coaxed. "A football. Tools."

While Pollard wasn't looking, Katie filched one of the white Christmas bells from the stack and slid it beneath a couch pillow.

Action figures? thought Matt. I'm not six years old. A football? Listen, if I were good enough for the team, I'd use the school's footballs. Tools? I don't want a wrench and a hammer. I want a laptop computer. Like anybody's going to fork over a thousand dollars for some foster kid's Christmas present.

Katie had one of those teachers who really got into Christmas. The third grade sang carols, and cut out snowflakes, and stood around admiring the teacher's angel collection.

Well, maybe there were angels, but neither Matt nor Katie had one.

Or else they had a defective angel who couldn't pull anything off.

Or else their angel didn't think they were worth much attention and had moved on to better kids.

It was easier to believe there were no angels.

"How about you, Katie?" said Pollard. He was filling out Matt's bell with blue jeans sizes.

The paper was so rich, it seemed as if he should be using a special pen, not a ninety-eight-cent ballpoint.

Matt let himself pretend that somebody would go out there and buy him a leather jacket. Tack had a leather jacket. Matt had not touched it, hanging in the restaurant coatroom, but he wanted to; the leather looked buttery soft, and the lining didn't look cold and slippery, like the lining in Matt's secondhand jacket, but velvety. It hung exactly right on Tack.

Katie was staring at the paper bell with her name on it as if she had just entered another world.

Matt could identify the shape and color of Katie's expression, and it was Hope. The hope took hold of her face, like loving hands on each cheek. She opened her eyes wider and wider, until Matt felt as if he could see into her soul.

The whole idea of Christmas presents, presents just for her, presents chosen and wrapped just for her, became bright gold, full of ribbons and stars.

"Pick out whatever you want, Katie," said Pollard carelessly, popping the point of the pen in and out.

"Whatever I want," Katie repeated softly.

The edges of the bell silhouette were deep and strong. You could almost hear the bell ring.

People who cut their wishing bells out of such expensive paper must be serious. This wasn't typing paper; wasn't scrap paper. It was heavy, like something legal, or the pages of a library book you weren't allowed to use. Red or green bells would have been more Christmassy, but white was a document that counted.

It felt real.

Possible.

"What do you want, Katie?" said Pollard, losing patience. "What do you really want for Christmas?"

Katie had flattened her palms against each other and was resting her fingertips against her chin. A trembling wondering expression—not a smile, not joy, but belief—contained both her face and her hands.

"I want a family," said Katie.

Great kings have precious gifts and we have naught

✦

Matt sucked in his breath and held on to the magazine pages.

Katie believed.

That was the thing he hated about this social work stuff, this promise stuff: little kids might believe.

Matt pressed his jaws together hard, a technique that gave him a shot of pain racing toward his eye and made stuff real.

Katie was beautiful.

Belief had made her happy; happiness made her lovely.

But Katie was way too old. Nobody ever said, "Oh, goodie, think I'll adopt an eight-year-old."

But he pictured it anyway. Like an old movie on a black-and-white cable station: a family rising from behind the tree, smiling and holding out their arms. All that invisible stuff that didn't go inside wrapping paper and boxes: comfort and love and niceness. Hugs and laps and—

Pollard shook his head. He adorned his face with his tightest smile. This was his signal that he was the adult who had the answers. "Christmas isn't about big things, Katie," said Pollard, chuckling. "It's about little things. Think little."

Matt thought of Liz and Jamie and Tack, for whom presents poured. He thought of Liz after she read his statement, "There is no Santa," regarding him with disturbing deepness, as if she saw down his mind. He thought of Jamie, paying no attention; and of Tack, smiling his eternal smile, as if life were good.

Matt was overwhelmed by the desire for Santa to be real. For Katie to have Santa.

"Think little," said Pollard again, tapping his pen the way Mrs. Wrenn tapped her nails.

Katie faded like an old sheet, as if she'd been washed too many times. Her hands came down slowly, and she sat on them, squishing out hope. She pressed her lips anxiously together, trying to think little. "A radio?" she said.

Pollard got annoyed.

"A plain one," added Katie quickly. "Ordinary."

"That plays cassettes," said Matt. "And a cassette to start with. A Christmas story tape." Christmas stories were always warm; there were grandmothers, and fireplaces, and stars.

Pollard made an exaggerated face, inverting his mouth, opening his eyes, squinching his nose. Matt wanted to beat Pollard to a pulp. "Worth a try," said Pollard, "worth a try."

Katie and Matt watched his pen move.

Katie—age 8—wants a radio/cassette player and a Christmas story tape.

48

On Christmas Day in the morning

✦

Matt worked hard at River Wind Inn that night.

He ignored Tack.

He ignored Tack's father.

When he had finished his own work, he pitched in to help with everybody else's.

Tack's father thanked him.

Matt shrugged.

Mr. Knight drove Matt home, and Matt said nothing to him, not good-bye, not thank you. He just got out of the car, slammed the door, and went into the Rowens' house.

Mrs. Rowen was still at the computer, typing and listening to her Christmas CDs. Mr. Rowen was watching the history channel. The sounds of World War II bombers blended with keyboard clicks and "Joy to the World."

Katie was still up. She was coloring at the kitchen table. Nothing would make her go to bed before everybody else. Up to the last possible moment, Katie wanted company.

Pollard's visit had wrecked Matt's homework schedule. He sat next to Katie and did his math. Numbers always did the right thing in the end. You could count on them.

Katie set down her crayons.

"What are you going to do with the bell you took?" Matt asked.

49

"Keep it." Katie had an old canvas carry bag with a single heavy-duty snap at the top, and in that open bag, Katie kept her few possessions. Matt had examined them once. Nothing worth anything, but she loved her bag and everything in it, and Matt knew how that was.

She had hidden the paper bell beneath her crayon page, but she had not colored it. He knew that she never would, because in its clean snowy way, it was a wish that could not fail her—because she was not using it.

Suddenly, in the hot resentful way Matt felt toward his mother, Katie was related to him. She was a sister, and he an older brother.

"Here, Katie," said Matt. "I'll fill it out the way you wanted." He took his own cheap ballpoint pen from the plastic zip bag inside his notebook, and he wrote across the stolen bell just the way Pollard had.

Katie, age 8, wants a family.

Her hair had fallen out of its ponytail. When she took the bell back from him and bent over it, her hair fell forward and hid her expression. Her fingertips slipped over the words, as if it were Braille and she could read through her skin.

There is no such thing as false hope, thought Matt, no matter what Pollard says. Hope just is. Every morning, every night. Hope doesn't guarantee. Hope doesn't promise. Hope doesn't do a thing.

But you have to have it.

He realized then that he did have hope; the Rowens

had given it to him; and even if he lost the Rowens, he had to hang on to hope.

And if Katie was his sister, for even one short hour on a Thursday night, he had to give her some of that hope.

"Because it isn't true!" said Matt fiercely. "Christmas *is* about big things." I'm lying, he thought. I have no idea what Christmas is about. Only people like Tack and Liz know what Christmas is about.

Katie was pretty again: the Katie who could be, should be, loved by somebody. "At school, Matt," she whispered, "some of the kids really *believe* in Christmas."

Neither Matt nor Katie knew what that meant. What was there to believe in? What was in this month of December that mattered?

She doesn't know what it is, thought Matt, *and she believes.*

This is wrong. I can't do this. She's too desperate. She believes. She thinks it will happen. I need to rip up the stupid bell and throw it away.

He said, "I'll hang your bell on the tree at River Wind."

Katie took a breath so deep it lifted her shoulders, raised her elbows, and spread her thin sweater. "Oh, Matt!" she whispered, and now everything about her gleamed: her eyes, her skin, her hair, her lips; and he had the terrifying thought that this was what angels looked like.

"Somebody will choose my bell, Matt!" Katie was laughing now, the first real laugh he had ever heard from her, the first normal natural laugh of delight. "Somebody will choose me for Christmas!"

51

O Christmas tree, O Christmas tree

Liz's mother had been baking Christmas cookies all day long. The house was full of cookies: bar cookies, spritz cookies, chocolate cookies, lace cookies, frosted cookies. A person who spends the entire day in the kitchen is too tired to make dinner, so the Kitchells were going out to River Wind Inn.

River Wind was both elegant and cozy. Each dining room had a fireplace, and there was something antique about having dinner in a room with a roaring fire. It felt wintry and right.

There was a wait, even though the Kitchells had a reservation. The outer room was hot and crowded. A fat short tree took up too much space. When people squeezed past, their winter coats brushed against the needles, and the room smelled of Christmas coming.

Liz's mother was not impressed by the decorations River Wind had used on its tree: a batch of identical white paper bells dangling on gold thread. Liz could tell her mother itched to do the tree over.

While Mom had been baking, Liz had been on the phone with her sister. "Allison, you have to come home for Christmas," she had said over and over. "How are we going to celebrate without you?"

"What is there to celebrate?"

"Us," said Liz. "Our family. Our love."

Her sister was ten years older than Liz. It meant they had not shared childhood, just parents. It meant that by the time Liz was old enough to have a real conversation on subjects that mattered, her sister was long gone—at college; getting married.

"I bought new packs of silver rain," Liz offered her sister.

Both sisters loved hanging tinsel on the Christmas trees. Liz would grab a handful of tinsel and hurl it toward an empty branch, and whether it was lumpy or graceful, Liz was done. Allison would open the little cardboard package with great care, then separate the strands and hang them one by one. It took her so long that Liz started to hope she'd just eat the rest and die a hideous death.

Allison said, "I didn't buy a Christmas tree. Daniel went and got one by himself."

Daniel was Allison's husband. It was strange to have a brother-in-law, especially one as old as Daniel. He was thirty, with the start of a bald spot. He did not feel like a brother to Liz, but like another father. In fact, Allison said she'd married him because she knew he'd be such a good father. The trouble was, you couldn't be a father of any kind unless you had a kid.

It was awful to picture Daniel going alone to pick out a tree. It was always such fun, so important, and yet so silly, and you should never have to do it alone.

"Listen, Allison," said Liz, "you have to come home for Christmas. Mom and Dad are being selfish and awful and they're doing nothing but shopping and I don't even like them this year." She didn't like herself either, talking like that. "I need you and Daniel to be the good guys. What kind of Christmas morning will it be without good guys?"

"I suppose I'm still a good guy," said Allison. "But life hasn't been good to me this year, Liz. I don't know how much Christmas spirit I can come up with."

"More than Mom and Dad," said Liz. Why am I talking about what I need? she thought. It's Allison who needs.

"Liz, Mom and Dad are the most Christmassy people in America," protested Allison.

"Maybe. But are you coming, Allison?"

"Daniel wants to. I'm still thinking."

The Kitchells moved up in line. Liz examined the bells on the restaurant tree. On each delicately cut white paper bell was handwriting.

> Rosie, age 7, wants a
> Slumber Party Barbie and
> Barbie bedsheets.

What is this? thought Liz. She slipped between two elderly women to get closer to the tree, and she read another bell.

> Dwayne, age 14, wants
> Nike Air Flight Max sneakers, size 10.

"What is this?" Liz's father demanded, yanking Dwayne's bell toward his bifocals.

Liz cringed. Dad loathed people who did not pay their

bills. He had little use for charity. He did not write checks for soup kitchens and he did not empty his wallet to help build a new playground and he did not contribute to hospices. He said God helped those who helped themselves, the only context in which he had ever mentioned God.

The headwaiter turned, and it had to be Tack. He wore a starched white shirt with a crisp collar and a Christmas vest, scarlet and gold, like a box of decorations brought down from the attic. His name tag was a gold Christmas tree, which said TACK in red glitter.

"Hey! Kitchells!" said Tack, grinning his old-man grin, with the long happy lines. "Welcome to River Wind."

Liz's smile burst out in return. "What are these bells?" she asked.

"Dad's idea," said Tack. Tack always sounded as if his life had just started off that morning and the sun was shining and somebody else had made breakfast. "They're Christmas wish bells. Gives everybody a chance to be Santa."

Liz loved the idea of everybody's getting a chance to be Santa.

"You guys haven't been dining here in December," teased Tack, "or you'd have seen them before. We've been doing restaurant trees for years. It includes three other restaurants now, so it's quite a job, and the church youth group took it over."

Tack had never spoken of church, youth group, or restaurant trees, in any paragraph read aloud in Mrs. Wrenn's class. "Are you in the youth group?" Liz asked.

"Yep," he said.

She liked how he said yep, like a cartoon character.

"And who are these names?" asked her father in his least pleasant voice.

"Kids," said Tack happily. "Kids who need a Santa. Their names come from teachers, day care, community center, welfare, the Y, stuff like that. Your job is to pick out a wish bell, buy the presents, wrap them, and take them to the church office before December twenty-third. Then the youth group distributes them."

"Our *job*?" said Liz's father. "Excuse me? We go out to eat at an expensive restaurant and get assigned a job?"

"Daddy," whispered Liz. She tugged on his sweater sleeve. Sometimes if she behaved like a five-year-old, he'd remember to behave like a grown-up.

Tack was courteous. "Some people do feel that way, sir. Not everybody wants to give."

Liz tried to give Tack a smile that would be flirty, apologize for her father, and yet also stick up for him— but there was no such smile.

"Last year," Tack confided, "we had ten bells left by Christmas, and those ten kids didn't get anything. But the year before, every single bell was taken by mid-December. We're hoping for a bare tree." He grinned. "I'm a Lego man myself. I go through the bells to see if some little guy asks for Legos, and somebody always does, and I buy him a big set, and sometimes I even get some for myself, because you can never have too many Legos."

Liz loved him completely, because he was right about Legos and because he gave presents to strangers.

"What a marvelous idea!" cried a woman behind the Kitchells. She was fat and unkempt, the kind of person who offended Liz's parents. Her blouse gaped open between the buttons and Liz was embarrassed for her. The woman pushed through, beaming widely to excuse herself, and read out loud from the bells. "Oh, Erin!" she said, yanking her little girl over Liz's father's shoes. "Isn't this perfect! Look! Here's a bell for some little girl named Rosie who's just your age, Erin, and wants just what you do! Barbie stuff. Let's us get Rosie's Christmas presents. Tomorrow we'll go on a Barbie spree." Mother and daughter both jumped up and down.

"How do you know," said Liz's father, "that there really is a Rosie? How do you know you're not supplying some social worker's kid with a larger Barbie collection?"

Tack nodded several times, as if he'd prepped for this question. "At least two adults—you know, caseworkers, teachers—have to agree that this kid won't have presents under the tree unless strangers do it."

Liz was as bad as her parents, thinking that the Neediest lived inside the television. But they lived here, and these were their names, and they didn't have presents on Christmas. And they were children.

Tack seated a party of six while Liz and the fat woman and little Erin read more tags. Liz had pretty well decided on Dwayne. She read Dwayne's bell out loud. " 'Dwayne, age fourteen,' " she said to her parents, " 'wants Nike Air Flight Max sneakers.' Those are the cool kind, with little windows in the soles, like a carpenter's level. They're orange on the inside and have a really neat tread pattern."

"They should make these kids ask for sensible stuff," said Liz's father. "Put it back, Liz. This is blackmail."

But Liz thought of Dwayne. She could picture Dwayne perfectly: his height, weight, color, eyes, smile, personality. Dwayne really wanted four presents, or a hundred, but nobody would get him that much. What to ask for? This was not a small decision. He picked the very best in sneakers, so at last, on Christmas morning, he'd have something his whole class would envy.

Her father swore. "What do designer sneakers like that cost? A hundred dollars? Maybe a hundred fifty!"

The mother of Erin had carefully taken Rosie's bell from the tree, and little Erin was holding the bell in both hands, as if it might escape. Erin was very short, lost beneath other people's elbows and winter coats. She wore that special frown of small children wanting to get the details exactly right. "Do I get to wrap Rosie's Barbies?" she said anxiously.

"Absolutely," said her mother. "You know, if we look hard enough, I bet we can find Barbie paper and a Barbie card."

Liz loved Erin's mother. What difference did it make if her blouse didn't fit?

"And Barbie stickers!" cried Erin. Erin and her mom were going to do this right, and they needed stickers.

Oh, Rosie, age seven, thought Liz. You're going to have presents under the tree. With stickers too.

Under the tree. Such a peculiar phrase. But so important to Liz. And Rosie. And Dwayne.

"It isn't blackmail, Dad," said Liz.

"Of course it is! We're at the town's most expensive restaurant, so they figure along with dinner, wine, and tip, we might as well buy some welfare kid Christmas presents. There's a time and a place to ask, and this isn't it."

Liz wondered. Was there really a time and a place for asking? Shouldn't all times and all places be okay for asking?

"I'm thinking of painting the living room again, did I tell you?" asked her mother. "I think it needs more passion. The interior wall needs to be deep plum, like the sofa."

"Jesus Christ, look at this!" exclaimed her father.

Considering that Liz lived in a house that had a dozen, or maybe a hundred, representations of Jesus right now, she knew not a single thing about him. Who was the guy, and why had anybody cared for two thousand years?

"Some sixteen-year-old wants a ski package!" Her father swore some more. "These are supposed to be charity cases! A ski package! That takes nerve. These people supposedly need my tax dollars to buy a loaf of bread, and now these freeloaders think they deserve a ski weekend from me too?"

> Azintra, age 16, wants the
> weekend ski package to
> Bear Mountain with the
> high-school ski club,
> on Presidents' Weekend.

59

Azintra, thought Liz. How many people can there be with that name? She must be the Azintra in my gym class!

Azintra was from some romantic distant place like Azerbaijan or Ukraine. Her parents worked twenty-four hours a day, as far as Liz could tell, running a bakery. Azintra had to work there the way Tack had to work here. But Azintra didn't get paid; it was just part of keeping the family afloat. Liz had never seen Azintra in the drink line at the cafeteria; never a Coke or a milk or an apple juice. Azintra drank water from the fountain. Azintra bought her clothing at the hospital thrift shop: two blouses for a dollar.

Of course Azintra wanted the ski weekend. She wanted friends, the long bus trip north, sleeping in the dorms of mountain housing, sharing the ski lift.

Liz was torn. She'd been all ready to give Dwayne his sneakers, so that he could bound into class and show off a little; but she didn't know Dwayne, and she did know Azintra. Could I give Azintra the ski trip? she worried. Do I have enough birthday money left? But then what about Dwayne? I don't want Dwayne to be one of the ten leftover bells.

"No," said Liz's father, reading her intention. "Aside from the fact that sixteen-year-olds are too old for Santa Claus, it is not appropriate to ask for a ski weekend."

"But Mommy," asked Erin, "who exactly is Rosie? Do we get to meet her? Will she know I sent the Barbies?"

"No," said her mother, "the presents will be from Santa."

Erin nodded, satisfied with this and understanding fully.

Erin's seven, thought Liz, and she knows who Santa is. *It's her*. When Erin wakes up Christmas morning, she'll know she did a good thing in the world.

What will we know, Christmas morning?

Lullay, thou little tiny child

✧

Christmas was about babies.

One baby.

It was about birth.

Allison's baby had been born, but had died.

Allison did not want Christmas. At Christmas there would be no escape from the baby: Mary's baby, Allison's baby. Allison felt that this Christmas, either the Star would never come, or it would come cold and cruel. Allison hated God. She woke up hating him, she hated him all day, and she fell asleep hating him.

Her husband, Daniel, said, "But Allison. You don't believe in God."

This was true. She had never believed in God. She had been brought up in a family that thought religion was pathetic and God did not exist.

I must be the strongest believer of all time, thought Allison, because I am so mad at God.

"Allison, come on," said Daniel. "We have to have a normal life again."

How were people whose baby had died ever supposed to be normal?

Allison was mad at anybody who had well children now, and among the people who got to have well children were Joseph and Mary, who every single year, for two thousand years, showed up with their kid in that stable.

Allison Kitchell had loved her childhood, and her plan was to duplicate it perfectly. She would marry the perfect man; they would buy the perfect house in the perfect town, have perfect children, and never move. Nothing would ever be thrown out; instead they would have a museum of their lives: every paper, every scrap of fabric, every clay handprint of their children.

Allison had wanted a baby ever since she could remember.

Back when she was a brand-new baby-sitter, only ten, her very first baby-sitting job was for a little boy named Ronald. Such an adorable baby needed a better name than Ronald, and Allison Kitchell held the sleeping infant in her arms, listing boys' names that were better than Ronald: "Michael, David, Kenny, Jon. Aaron, Alex, Nicholas, Sam."

Allison began planning for her baby right then.

She and Daniel began dating when Allison was in high school and he was in college, and she told Daniel they were going to get married and have lots of kids, and Daniel said he hadn't really thought about it much, and Allison explained that she would make the decisions.

When she was eighteen, she wanted to get married and have a baby, and everybody said, "No no no no no no no, you're too young, finish school, have a career, save lots of money. Then have a baby."

Allison waited as absolutely long as she possibly could. Finally, when she was twenty-one, she said, "Daniel, I can't wait any longer, I want a baby." Daniel thought they should wait.

They waited about half an hour, and then Daniel said, "Okay, fine, let's go to a justice of the peace and get married and start this baby," so they did.

Allison's parents and Daniel's parents went nuts. They'd wanted a great big wedding. Allison had always meant to have a great big wedding, too, having bought every brides' magazine in the world for years, but somehow it didn't matter that she'd skipped it.

Then they didn't have a baby.

They didn't, and they didn't, and they didn't.

So Allison finished college, and Daniel started a company that did huge special events, like rock concerts, and the next thing they knew they had a ton of money, and then they had a baby.

For four days, they had a baby.

That was a short time.

And the baby died.

That would be a long time. That would be every minute that Allison lived. Every day of her life, she would be a mother whose baby had died. A baby who never had a first Christmas, or a first tooth, or a first step.

"I don't even want a Christmas tree this year," said Allison to her husband, and Daniel said, "Allison. Please. *Stop this. I need you.*"

She looked at him and saw that it was true. He needed her, and she had to stop this.

O God! she said in her heart, and it was not swearing; it was praying. She had prayed for only one thing in her life—that her baby would live. The prayer had not been answered. O God, she prayed, let me not be so angry. Let me be here for Daniel.

And it happened.

As if she had blown out candles on a birthday cake, her wish, or her prayer, came true. She was not so angry. She was there for Daniel.

It happened in two words: *O God.* She was amazed and almost frightened. She said to him miserably in her heart, So, God: So where were you when the baby was sick?

Her sister, Liz, called and said, "Allison, I need you home for Christmas."

It was good to be needed. And Allison could not imagine how you faced the end of the year without Christmas. You needed December; it was the crown.

Need, she thought. I need my baby still. I need to take care of somebody. I want to spend my life taking care of somebody. And I love Daniel, and he does need me, and I love my sister and my parents, and they do need me, but—

The only person who had really needed Allison had needed more than Allison could give. More than modern medicine could give. And that person was very small and light and wrapped forever in a little blanket Allison had knit when she was happy.

So Allison said, "You're right, Liz, and we'll be home for Christmas. Say hi to Mom and Dad." And then she hung up fast, because the only person Allison wanted to say hi to could no longer hear her voice.

Peace to all that have goodwill

✦

Matt had let himself be escorted to math practice, like a girl to a dance. "Math team isn't so bad, Matt," said Tack. "Sometimes it's kind of fun. Anyway, we need you."

The team did not use first names. There was no Matt, Tack, Candice, or Jed. They were Morden, Knight, Piero, and MacBurn. "Sounds like a law firm," said Mrs. Simmetti. "Morden, Knight, Piero, and MacBurn. You guys have to stay together; you'll look good on a plaque."

Staying together was not what foster kids did.

But the four names danced in Matt's mind, like tap shoes: Morden, Knight, Piero, and MacBurn.

Matt was more anxious about the meet than he could allow Tack to know. Tack just didn't get anxious about anything. Matt believed this was because Tack had a father.

According to Matt's mother—as if Matt could trust her in any way, including the history of his birth—a marriage had existed, and been good, and even had things like a paid-for car that ran, and supper on the table. But his father died, said his mother, died in a stupid accident on a construction site, died pointlessly, and died completely.

That was the thing: the completeness of it. Matt had had a whole life, and no father in it anywhere.

66

He did not blame his mother's collapse into drugs and crime on the dead father, because who knew? And what was the point of blame, anyway? But he thought of the dead father sometimes, and his thoughts were as pointless as that death; they didn't take him anywhere; they didn't solve anything.

When Matt saw the Knight family—and this included Tack's mother, who was the banquet manager; but Matt never permitted himself thoughts of mothers, because he had one, technically; and mothers like his could not be thought of—but when Matt saw them, so strong and certain, he was overwhelmed with how they knew so easily, every day, every evening, where they were going and what they were doing.

The night after the first math practice, Candice Piero and Jed MacBurn and a bunch of other kids gathered at River Wind Inn. They and Tack and Mr. Knight hung the wish bells on the restaurant tree. They were all members of the church youth group. Everybody, Tack explained to Matt, belonged to the church youth group.

Everybody, thought Matt.

Clubs had always given Matt muscle spasms, and that kind of club was just as bad. Okay, fine, call it a church, but what it really was, was a club. Only clubs used the word *belong*. Only clubs said "everybody" when they really meant "us." Only certain kinds of people went there, and only in certain circumstances. Matt wasn't the type and didn't know the rules. Nor had he ever lived with anybody who was or did.

The next day in school, he said to Tack, "Whaddaya do in that youth group?"

"Nothing," said Tack.

A true club. The members never miss a meeting, but they pretend it doesn't matter and isn't anything.

Matt never wanted to speak to Tack again. He did not want to go to math team, or practice with him, or work with him at the restaurant. He felt enormously tired, as if he were an autumn leaf and his season were over. He felt ready to fall from the branch.

Matt had not trusted the restaurant tree, but people were taking the bells. They'd coo, and exclaim, and even clap, and get all excited about being Santa. They would actually thank Mr. Knight for letting them have this chance. Many bells were already gone.

When he wandered past the tree and hung Katie's wish, he felt like a fool. But Matt found himself hoping—

Well, he didn't hope for a family for Katie. He knew she couldn't get that. And yet—

He wanted her bell up there.

He wanted the wish to have a chance.

He thought: I'm the one who still wants a family. I still want my mother to get well, and my father to be alive and be just like Tack's father.

And none of these wishes would ever come true.

But Katie—

Whenever Mrs. Rowen gave Matt a ride to work, Katie would hop in the backseat and come along. She'd beg permission to run inside with him, pretending she wanted to see the pretty decorations. She'd circle the tree. If a bell had been taken, she'd scoot into the kitchen to whisper the news to Matt: "Noreen and Jason are going to get their presents, Matt!" and they would actually smile at each other, and there would be this link between them, and the link was a present given by a stranger to a stranger.

And the link was a secret: only Matt and Katie knew about Katie's wish.

The night Liz's family came to the restaurant, Matt tried to stay out of sight. His bibbed apron was wet and stained, and his hair was sweaty. But he admired Liz's family from the kitchen door. Her parents were beautiful, the way he had known they would be. Their clothes were right, and their hair, and Liz's father looked like an attorney or a broker. Born in a suit, probably, his whole life tailored and smooth.

Mr. Kitchell's hand moved to the wish tree, and his fingers caught a golden thread, removing a wish bell. Whose wish? thought Matt, who had them all by memory.

He felt suddenly warm toward the world, even toward Christmas. It was such a strange feeling; right against his chest, like a hot-water bottle a foster parent had given him once when he had the flu.

From the rich to the poor
they are mostly unkind

✦

Liz could not stop reading the bells.

> Ryan, age 6, wants action toys,
> a baseball mitt, and Matchbox cars.

> Lori, age 4, wants a baby doll
> with hair she can comb.

> Katie, age 8, wants a family.

Liz stepped back from that one.

> Katie, age 8, wants a family.

It was chilling. It made her hair prickle and her palms damp.

"Look at that!" said her father, stabbing his finger against the same bell. "Katie, age eight, wants a family? That is *evil*. I don't care what good intentions Tom Knight has. I don't care how saintly those church people think they are. It is evil to pretend to some little kid that she's going to find a family under her Christmas tree. I can see asking for a doll if they can prove this little girl won't have presents otherwise. But *this*—it's an outrage! Hey, they want this kid to have a family, why don't they supply the family? Why expect some innocent person going out for dinner to cry, 'Oh, yes, just what I want to do; be a family to an eight-year-old.' "

"Somebody might," said Liz, praying for a table.

Mom was an old hand at not looking related to Dad when he was crabby in public. She drifted away, as unattached to the scene Dad was making as she was to everything else.

"You believe in miracles, then," said Liz's father.

"They aren't trying for miracles, Dad. They're just trying to give a Barbie to a little girl."

"Okay, the Barbie she can have. But this—" Liz's father had been stabbing his index finger at the bell that asked for a family. Now he closed his fingers around it and yanked. The gold cord did not come free. Needles spilled to the floor. He untangled the little thread and had the bell in his hand.

He ripped the bell in half.

Then he ripped the halves in half and threw them in the wastebasket behind the reservation desk.

For all weary children, Mary must weep

·★·

Matt was not actually surprised, because life was like that. But he had to duck back into the kitchen fast. It took all his control to scrape dishes instead of smash them. When Tack spoke to him, Matt wanted to snarl, hit, kick. *You and your stupid tree!* Every muscle in his body knotted, and the pain in his gut spread to his back, which was rare; usually he could contain the rage a little more easily.

"What is your problem?" demanded Tack.

Matt dropped the plate he was scraping. He doubled his right hand into a fist and drew it back.

Mr. Knight stepped between them. Matt's fist was moving, but he managed to prevent it from colliding with Mr. Knight.

"Tack, leave the kitchen," said his father. "Matt, come outside with me."

He didn't mean outside the kitchen, he meant outside, where it was snowing again, very lightly. The air was soft, and there was little wind.

Mr. Knight put his arm around Matt's shoulder, but Matt stepped away.

He did not know why, since what he most wanted on this earth was that very arm; an arm resting against him in comfort, not anger.

"Talk to me, Matt," said Mr. Knight, but Matt had nothing to say.

They were used to the heat and steam of the kitchen. It was probably only thirty degrees, but they were both shivering. Matt tried to step into his army dream, with the uniform and the distance, but he couldn't get there, and what he wanted most was to take one step closer to Mr. Knight, but it didn't happen.

He watched the snow layer gently on his sneakers.

"You okay now?" asked Mr. Knight finally.

Matt nodded.

They went back in. Tack wasn't around, and nobody seemed to have noticed anything, and Matt went on with the dishes. It was another half hour before Matt was calm enough to leave the kitchen, big gray plastic dish basin in his arms, and detour past the Christmas tree, and look in the wastebasket behind the reservation desk, where Mr. Kitchell had tossed the bell he had torn up.

The four pieces lay on top of crushed envelopes and used tissues. The words written on them had been separated, but not destroyed. It was his own handwriting. It was Katie's bell.

Never interfere, thought Matt. I broke the rule, I interfered, now Katie's going to pay.

He had let Katie down as cruelly as his own mother always let him down, and it killed him that breaking his rule of not connecting had led to this: he had connected Katie to a Christmas morning of nothing and nobody, when she was so sure her Christmas would be everybody, for always.

Matt went way past the mere smashing of dishes. It would be better to smash people, all these people. Smash every do-gooder in the world, including himself.

Katie would come along when Mrs. Rowen brought him tomorrow, and her bell would be gone, and she would believe.

He could tape up the torn bell, but among those bells so perfect and rich, Katie's would be obscene, with rough edges and overlaps and tape.

The bells were on special paper. He couldn't make another and substitute it.

He could tell Tack he needed a blank bell.

Yeah, right. Tack knew nothing of hope or pain, and Matt knew nothing of how to talk about them.

Go to the church office, somehow? Or the restaurant office? Would Mr. Knight keep spare wish bells lying on his desk? And if Matt got hold of a blank, so what? Matt would fill it out again, Katie would believe the lie again, and Matt would be the liar. Matt had insisted that Christmas was about big things.

Well, it wasn't.

He went back into the kitchen and stood over the enormous stainless-steel sink and held his hands under scalding hot water, and it hurt, and Matt wanted to hurt something back.

After a while, he remembered that only one thing mattered: pleasing the Rowens so that he could stay.

Katie didn't matter.

So Katie cried on Christmas morning, big deal, who cared? She'd been stupid to listen to him. He'd been stupid to bother.

Cold on his cradle

✦

Liz could not eat. The sauce was too rich, the spices too intense. Even the chocolate dessert was bitter.

She felt as if her father had damaged something sacred. And yet, the Kitchell family did not believe anything was sacred. The Kitchells did not believe there were special attributes in a piece of paper, whether it was a page from a Bible or a bell on a tree. Christmas itself felt ugly and torn. Pieces of what it should have been.

Her parents talked of wine, and whether the restaurant's wine list was good, and which wines they should offer their own guests at all the Christmas parties. Katie! thought Liz. We have to talk about Katie!

She felt like a loaf of bread, cut by a serrated knife, the crumbs of her falling to the bread board, to be swept away by a careless hand. Her parents noticed nothing. Maybe I'm just an ornament, too, she thought. I'm the decorative daughter, embroidered with high grades and good manners.

Tack's father was moving from table to table, saying hello, making sure everybody was happy with the dinner, comfortable with the music, pleased with the waiter. Liz hoped Mr. Knight would skip their table, because she did not want to hear her father's views on welfare kids again.

Anyway, they weren't all welfare. Azintra certainly

wasn't. She was just poor. She had no hope of participating in something like a ski weekend.

Unless I do it. But if I get Azintra the ski weekend, how can I get Dwayne his sneakers?

Her parents lingered over cappuccino, and finally they were done, and while Dad helped Mom with her coat, Liz wandered toward the reservation desk and bent down to fish the four torn pieces out of the wastebasket. Along the tears, the bells were not sharp like cut paper, but soft-edged as flannel. She slid them into her jacket pocket.

Whom shepherds guard and angels sing

✦

The floor was wet. Tack had to mop that up before somebody slipped. He was sick of restaurants. He was sick of the effort it took to be charming and delightful all evening long for your whole life. He hoped somebody would slip, preferably Matt.

"Just steer clear of him for the rest of the evening," Tack's father said calmly.

"But Dad, I set things up to get Matt to math practice; I prep everybody on the team like onions in the kitchen. Mrs. Simmetti guides him along like a satellite. And here, where we give him a job because you think it'll be good for his self-esteem and all, he's just an obnoxious jerk."

Tack loved math; he loved the shape and consistency of equations and calculations. He thought that people should behave like math and take their part in the equation. The restaurant trees were a nice math package: you put in a certain amount of work, people got a certain amount of excited, and you ended up with a certain amount of Christmas.

But not Matt, no. You could work on being nice to him all year, and you wouldn't end up with a certain amount of anything.

Tack's father could always take time out to be serious. Amid the rushing of waiters, the clamor of diners, the demands of the chef, his father said, "You don't do the right thing in order to have results, Tack. You do the right thing because it's right."

"Then how come Matt doesn't do the right thing? It's his turn!"

"He probably won't take a turn, Tack. He hasn't had that kind of life. I expect you to go on giving him a boost."

Tack shoved the mop furiously. "You go and you're nice to somebody, it's their turn."

His father shook his head. "You didn't sign a contract with Matt. He owes you nothing."

"Then how come I owe him?" demanded Tack.

"Because your mother and I brought you up that way."

Tack considered breaking the mop handle in half.

Sleep as they sleep who find their heart's desire

✦

Long after she should have been asleep, Katie liked to sit up in bed, staring out the window and down the steep hill at a distant highway, watching the headlights of cars. She never tired of those two rows: piercing white head-lights, ruby red taillights. All those people, always driving. All of them going home. Even at one in the morning, going home. She loved to watch their cars, go-ing home.

Me too, thought Katie. Going home.

When traffic was close enough to identify the vehicles, Katie would scan them closely. The family who chose her would have one of those high, heavy cars with four-wheel drive: the kind you filled with kids and dogs and ten bags of groceries. Katie would get to go grocery shopping and pick out her own cereal.

Morn, they called it, when it was Christmas. Other days were mornings. Christmas was Morn.

She loved the school bus ride now. So many cars to study. She would stare out the window. She loved the way the city looked in December. She loved going home to hope.

Excitement about Christmas had reached a fever pitch in third grade. Two kids were flying away—in air-planes!—to see their grandparents for Christmas. Two kids were getting puppies. They already knew. Jeannie was getting a cocker spaniel, and Mrs. Halsey had gotten out the encyclopedia and they had all looked at the picture of the cocker spaniel, and if Katie had ever seen a dog that would love you, this was the dog.

Kids were so excited they couldn't work; they couldn't talk about anything except Christmas. Katie did not dare talk about Christmas, for fear that a single misplaced word would keep the family from coming.

She tried to imagine how it would work. Her family wouldn't really be under a tree, like a present. Would they drive to the foster home? Or would they call? Would the social worker take Katie? Would she get there in time for lunch?

Katie sat up in the cold bedroom, smiling at the lights of families going home.

And one of them was hers.

The snow lay on the ground,
the stars shone bright

·✦·

Liz loved waking up. She usually woke up very early, around six, but wouldn't open her eyes for an hour. She liked that dozy feeling, when you knew your sheets and your pillow, your dreams of last night and your plans for the day, but you didn't explore them; you floated along the edge of your sleep, like a raft in a warm pool.

On Saturday, she snapped awake.

There was so much to do. Birthday money to get from the bank. The decision between Dwayne and Azintra. A bell to take off the restaurant tree. The bringing of that gift, wrapped and labeled, to the church for delivery.

Liz didn't have her driver's license yet, so she still did a lot of walking, and hers was an easy city to walk in. You just had to know which neighborhoods to avoid. There were a lot.

She dressed very warmly and set out.

It was cold, but not scary cold. Liz was afraid of intense cold. When it dropped to the low teens or single digits, when the wind was so bitter that the best-insulated house had cold spots and the warmest jacket wasn't warm, her thoughts got primitive. What if the car stalls on a back road and nobody comes by and we freeze to death? What if somebody's grandmother falls going out to get the newspaper and nobody sees her?

When she reached River Wind Inn, it was early for

lunch, and the place was open but empty. This was good. She did not want to see Tack in his Christmas vest, with his Christmas smile and his Lego habit. Liz walked up to the tree, took Azintra's bell, and left, safe in her secret good thing.

The bank was next. She was surprised at how much she enjoyed withdrawing the money. They gave it to her in crisp new twenty-dollar bills, and her heart soared like a ski lift, whipping Azintra to the top of the slope, in the midst of friends and snow.

Back home, she set the bills in a gift box, covering it in tissue that sparkled with stars and tying gold ribbons on it, using a little tool that slashed the ribbons into slender strips and turned them into a handful of stars. She wrote: *Happy skiing, Azintra. Love, Santa.*

I feel more love for Azintra than for my own parents, she thought. That's awful. I can't be that way. I want us to have a merry Christmas too.

It was funny how, before Christmas, you said to people, "Merry Christmas!" but after Christmas, you congratulated yourselves. "Good Christmas," you said to each other, nodding, because everything had been just right.

Could everything be just right again? The invasion of death was so complete. They had not known this baby: this four-day-old person who belonged to Daniel and to Allison. And yet the loss was huge, and constant, even for Liz.

Liz did not know how to help her sister, and she did not want to lose the bright and gleaming edges of doing good, so she skittered downstairs, trying to stay thrilled for Azintra, trying not to worry whether Dwayne got his sneakers, trying most of all not to think of an eight-year-old named Katie whose bell lay in four pieces in her jacket pocket.

She could not pretend that giving Azintra a ski trip canceled her father's ripping up that bell. The church group would be keeping count. If that little girl Katie's bell was gone, they would be expecting . . . what *could* they be expecting? Could they actually believe a family was going to appear?

Her father was almost right; they should not have that kind of wish up there—a wish that could never be fulfilled.

But they had, and so Liz had to get the bell replaced. How could she do that without admitting to Tack or Mr. Knight that her own father had shredded it?

Maybe she could pretend. "We took it home—and I'm not sure what we thought we could do—but we couldn't—it didn't work out—and so—here—it's yours again—except somehow I lost the bell on my way over."

Liz usually went down the stairs with her hand sliding on the slippery polished banister, but it was woven now with silk holly.

Christmas is so weird, thought Liz. It's weird to be bringing pieces of trees into the house and weaving them through the spaces of your handrails, but it's even weirder to make *fake* pieces of trees and weave those through the spaces.

"Darling!" cried her mother. "Allison called with her

flight number. She and Daniel will fly in December twenty-third, so we'll have a perfect Christmas after all. We'll all be here!"

How extraordinary, thought Liz. We won't all be here. Allison and Daniel's baby—my niece—your first grand-child—she won't be here. How will it be perfect?

"I just love going to the airport on a holiday," said her mother. "Everybody else in the world is there, too, and you do those special airport hugs, and you're part of a warm perfect world."

Liz nodded. She wondered what Allison was going to say if her mother babbled like this.

"At Christmas," said her mother, hugging Liz tightly, "once everybody gets home, it feels as if they never left. The family always fits right back together."

She is one of the neediest, thought Liz. She needs me, and Allison, and a hug, and a thousand more hugs. I'm the one who is selfish and small.

Katie, age eight, wants a family.

Who wrote that? Who allowed it to go up? Who was this child, and was anything going to fit together for her on December twenty-fifth?

"Where are you going, darling?" asked her mother.

"Shopping," said Liz, and to make sure that Mom didn't try to come along, she said, "Secret stuff. See you later."

She plowed across the wide yards, leaving a trench of boot prints in the snow. Both her house and the church had a lot of land, and she loved being the first to walk there. She had never actually been inside the church. Or

84

any church. She was surprised to see how much the hall and office looked like a school. Boring, and in need of paint.

She knocked on the office door, and although it was a Saturday, somebody was there.

Tack.

She did not want to see him, never mind talk to him. But there was no way to avoid speech. "I have a bell present," she said.

"Great! That's what I'm working on right now. Get a plain grocery bag from that stack over there, stick your present in it, staple the bell onto the bag, staple the bag shut. If it's fragile, put it in the pile on the shelf, not the floor."

Liz put her present on the flat bottom of the brown paper bag. She liked stapling the bell on, closing the bag up. It felt accomplished. Like mailing a letter: it was on its way now. Azintra was really going skiing.

She wanted to ask about Katie, age eight, who wanted a family. She wanted to say—Who let Katie's bell go up?

She wanted to say—My father says it's evil, so he tore it up. She wanted to say—My whole family is torn up, how's yours?

She said, "Are enough people choosing bells?"

"Pretty much," said Tack. "We've got three other trees this year. Lobster Catch, Benny's Pizza, and Le Chocolat. They're such different places. Guess we'll find out if people who want a pepperoni pizza will take more or fewer bells than people who want a white chocolate truffle with raspberry sauce."

"What happens to the bells nobody picks?"

Tack shook his head and shrugged. "We raise money all year with car washes and bake sales and stuff. We have our own treasury, which means the youth group can fill a few of them, and my parents and some other parents try to do what's left, but some of 'em—you can't do it. They don't get their presents."

He smiled, but it was not his wonderful grin; it was quiet and old. "When we take the lost wishes down from the tree, it's awful. Like a sacrifice. But some of them, you know already it's not going to work. Like Dwayne on our tree. Dwayne is not going to get any hundred-dollar pair of sneakers."

Liz stared at the rows of brown paper pyramids.

Lost wishes.

The office door was flung open, whacking against the wall, slightly increasing the diameter of a hole in the plaster, and Mr. Knight came in. "Hey, Liz!" he said, as if he'd been yearning to run into her. "How're we doing, Tack?"

"Pretty good. Donny gets his Y membership so he can swim."

"You mean, you know these kids?" said Liz. "You know Donny?"

Tack looked embarrassed.

"We don't know any of them," said Mr. Knight. "But you get to know your bells, and you root for them."

Liz skated near the torn bell problem. "So what about the kids who don't get their wishes?" she asked. "Do you notify the caseworker?"

"First," said Tack, "we run through the restaurant and

86

strangle all the people who haven't done their share." He
made this sound like such fun that Liz wanted to volun-
teer, except the strangle-ees would include her own father
and mother.

"Yes, Liz," said Mr. Knight, "we call the referrals.
They're hard calls."

Liz made a hard call. She said, "Thank you for letting
me participate. Merry Christmas."

"Merry Christmas, Liz," they said back, and they did
not know, and she would never tell them, about the torn
bell of Katie, age eight.

Oh, rest beside the weary road

⋆

Rick Pollard had been a social worker more than half his life. He had gone into this profession because he thought he could change things for the better, but that didn't happen.

The harder he worked, the more cases they gave him, and pretty soon he could hardly tell one kid from another, and the calendar was so full he couldn't fit them all in anyway.

His life was a schedule, broken down by the quarter hour: rush here, drive here, fill out this form, make that phone call, double-check this, be sympathetic, arrange for a specialist . . .

He understood the Rowens. He felt the same.

There were some kids who gave you no reward. Kids who were just there, demanding more. Katie, whose mother had been in prison all Katie's life, had no personality. She might be capable of it; her first foster family had had her for three years, and supposedly a kid's ability to love and to be loved came from those early years. But that family had suddenly had twins of their own, and the foster children had been dispersed into the system, and Katie had failed.

Katie believed that first foster mother was her real mother; Katie had decided against remembering what she had been told plenty of times—that Mom was in prison.

Katie couldn't hear that. In fact, Katie couldn't hear a lot of things. He'd had her tested for deafness, but there was nothing wrong with Katie's ears. Just her heart.

As for Matt, the kid had a chance. Not a great one. But if they could keep him off drugs—which wasn't likely; you had a parent whose life was addiction, you probably had a kid whose life would be addiction—but Matt, frozen like a package of vegetables, a cold person who spoke little and touched never, Matt had discipline.

It was possible, though not likely, that Matt could survive his childhood. Whether he could ever be happy was something else.

And Pollard had learned in twenty sad years of social work in this sad hard city that only happy kids got loved. The rest got abandoned.

Nothing is so important as a happy childhood.

If you were hugged and held when you were little, if you were in the midst of laughter and love—hey; you'd probably be fine no matter what.

But if you were on your own, and without affection, without joy—hey; you'd probably fail no matter what.

He did not want a world like this; a world where people talked of stars but dealt in mud. But there was nothing he could do. That had been Rick Pollard's first, and most lasting, lesson: there is not enough love to go around.

He made a hard call. He got in his car and drove to the Rowens'.

Myrrh is mine; its bitter perfume
Breathes a life of gathering gloom

✦

Matt headed home from math practice. Tack had stopped trying to talk to Matt, and somehow that made it possible for Matt to go.

There was a late bus, an activity bus, but he didn't take it. Walking was solitary; you were okay when you were solitary.

It was cold out, but Matt rarely minded cold, and he wore no gloves. He liked to ball his hands up and stuff them in his jacket pockets, but the jacket was a size too small, so his fists ended up too high. Other guys wore a size too large; the small jacket marked him as somebody whose parents didn't bother.

The Rowens' house was on a hill, and Matt liked walking uphill. He liked the pull on his legs. He thought of math team, and he permitted himself an actual formed thought about the father he did not have. If Matt told him about math team, would his father care?

He could make up any father he wanted, but that real father, that one Matt could never know—would he be proud?

Pollard's car was in the Rowens' driveway.

Matt had forgotten Pollard.

Another unscheduled visit.

He could not believe it. It wasn't fair.

Not before Christmas.

Please.

He tried to laugh at himself. So look at you. You who didn't believe. *You believed. You hoped.*

He schooled himself to be expressionless, wordless. Hopeless.

He walked on, because it was always best to get it over with.

Peace on earth, and mercy mild

⋆

Liz had English homework, which was unusual for Mrs. Wrenn, who disliked having to take papers home to correct.

"Write a Christmas poem," Mrs. Wrenn had said. And to nobody's surprise, added, "Keep it short. As if you were writing a Christmas card. Two lines of verse on the outside, two on the inside."

Liz walked around the house examining the Christmas collections to give herself poem ideas. Her friend Rachel had been mildly annoyed by the Christmas card assignment, since Rachel celebrated Hanukkah, and had explained to Mrs. Wrenn that she would write something else. Since Mrs. Wrenn did not believe anything had meaning, Christian or Jewish, the correction bored her; she simply shrugged with her smile.

Rachel's house did not change much for Hanukkah. A menorah. Simple. There were candles. Did candle flame bring hope and light to Rachel? Did Rachel believe? Would she write a poem about it—or would she keep it to herself?

Liz fingered a fat green candle wrapped in wax holly, scented with pine. Her mother never lit the candles, preferring them pristine, with no dripping sides.

Perhaps Liz should choose trees.

Liz had never met a crummy Christmas tree.

There was something about the way trees lined themselves up at the Boy Scout lot, or stacked themselves beside the flower shop—they were all just right; green and true and sure.

But Liz could not write about trees, unless it was the restaurant tree. And that belonged to Tack.

Liz inspected her mother's three manger scenes: handblown crystal on the mantel, painted china on the long high table that ran behind the sofa, olive wood from Bethlehem in straw on the breakfast table.

In each Nativity scene, the Mary sat quietly. She never looked up to see the Wise Men, the Star, or the shepherds. Mary's eyes were always fixed on her baby.

Liz picked up the olive-wood Mary. She imagined the three kings bringing those beautiful ornaments to Baby Jesus; Mary saying to Joseph, What are we supposed to do with these? We don't even have a house, never mind a place to store ornaments. Our kid is in a manger, we need a real crib, and these guys are giving us frankincense and myrrh?

A manger! thought Liz, and she had her poem.

Her poem would be like Shel Silverstein, like *The Giving Tree,* and in her poem, too, a tree would be cut down, and it would cry,

Use my wood
For something good!

And Liz thought: Is this what we yearn for in our lives?

93

Is this the question Mrs. Wrenn ought to be asking us to write about?

To use our wood for something good? Not just to burn in the fire, not just to rot in the forest, but to build something: something good and something right?

Shepherds, why this jubilee?

✦

Matt got himself in the Rowens' door.

Everybody said, "Hi, Matt."

Matt said nothing. He looked for Katie and found her frozen in front of the television. He knew the feeling. TV you could count on. Any crummy people on TV were gone in half an hour. But real life—

Matt thought of real life.

"Are you listening, Matthew?" asked Pollard.

He could not nod. His spine would crack. He would be paralyzed.

"We're sorry," said Mr. Rowen. "It's just too much for us."

Katie was not even a person; she was a little mannequin, a plastic thing with painted skin, waiting to be taken apart, her limbs and head stored.

"We'll wait till after Christmas," said Mrs. Rowen. "So you'll still have Christmas here. But Mr. Pollard felt it wasn't good for you to have false hope. So he wants you to know now, so you can get ready."

Get ready, thought Matt. Get set. Go. Because that's always the point: going.

Mr. Rowen said, "Katie, honey, I'm real sorry. It isn't you. It's that—well, we were doing fine with Matt, and I'm afraid we can't handle two kids. And Matt, don't you blame yourself, it isn't you."

95

Their speech came from a distance, as if Matt were underwater, and when he tried to look at the Rowens, their faces and mouths wavered, and he was sinking.

"We decided," said Mr. Rowen, "to go back to being the three of us."

The swamp around Matt's brain drained. The three adults in the room acquired mass and weight. He was able to tell one from the other. "Three of us?" he asked. "You mean, I'm staying?"

"Yes," said Mr. Rowen. "We're very proud of how you're doing in school, Matt, and we don't want to disrupt that."

I'm staying. They're not moving me. It's only Katie.

He was swamped again, but with relief. He had to use the wall to stay upright. It was only Katie who was going.

Pollard leaned way forward to get his face close to Katie's face. Matt knew how scary it was when you were little: an authority face shoved in your own. Katie did not cringe, and Matt did not know if she was too shocked to move, or too tough.

"Do you have any questions, Katie?" asked Pollard.

Of course Katie had questions. But what was the point in asking? Pollard's car door would open, Katie would get in with her pitiful belongings, and the car would drive away, and when it stopped, she would get out. It would almost certainly not be this school district. She would not have Mrs. Halsey. She would not know any of the kids when class began again in January. She would have no friends. She would have failed again.

"But you'll be here Christmas morning, Katie," said Pollard. He straightened up and shifted gears into his big cheery voice. "You'll be glad to know that somebody chose your Christmas bell. You're going to get what you want for Christmas."

Katie's face turned to gold.

Her little arms lifted like an angel hearing great good news. She came to her feet, and joy filled out her body, giving her length and breadth.

The grown-ups began to fill out forms and discuss details, and Matt knew they actually believed Katie was this happy because she was going to get a little radio with a single cassette.

Katie hugged herself, because there was nobody else to do it.

Could it be a hug, Matt wondered, when there weren't two people?

She beamed at him, and in the air she traced a bell, including the ringer at the bottom and the gold loop at the top.

I did this. I hung Katie's bell on the tree. Her joy is my fault.

No, Katie! Matt wanted to scream, that's not the family they meant! You're just moving to a different foster home. You're getting a radio for Christmas, and that's it, Katie. Nobody wants you, that's what this all means. *Nobody wants you.*

He hated himself because he was glad it was Katie losing her home, and not him.

There is such a thing as false hope, thought Matt. For Katie, all hope is false. All dreams, all beliefs.

But Katie doesn't know yet.

And all the flowers looked up at him
And all the stars looked down

❖

Katie darted from window to window, breathing hard. She misted up her own view and had to rub the glass panes clear with her hand. She welcomed the plows, watched the families come and go. Snow added skirts and capes to every bush. The street was so different from what it had been a few hours before.

Like me, thought Katie. I'll be different.

Other people were going to church on Christmas Eve. Katie had never done this. Mrs. Halsey went to church. She said there was a pageant.

Katie fell in love with that word. *Pageant.* If she had a girl doll, if her family gave her a really nice doll, Katie would call her doll Pageant.

Mrs. Halsey said it meant a long line—an indoor parade—everybody who was part of Christmas, and they would wear beautiful robes and sing beautiful songs, and there would be candles.

"Matt," whispered Katie.

He said nothing.

He had said nothing for days. It scared Katie. What if the Rowens kicked him out after all? He didn't have a family coming in the morning. What would happen to Matt?

Katie prayed for Matt, and she was amazed to find

that she knew how. She had never met God, but when she said, "God, Matt doesn't have a family coming in the morning! You have to take care of him!" she felt a lot better, as if someplace where Katie couldn't hear him doing it, God had said, "Sure, thanks for reminding me."

The church that Mrs. Halsey went to was so pretty: high up, with tall granite steps. It had a sky-piercing steeple full of swinging bells that chimed the hour. Katie liked the bells any time of day: she liked to wake up to the bells, she liked to fall asleep by them. The River Wind family—Tack and his parents—also went there. So the church was full of people Katie liked; it would be a safe place. And it would have that pageant thing, that thing she was going to name her doll for.

"Matt," said Katie, "let's go to that Christmas pageant they do at the church."

Matt and Katie had walked by the church many times. It was not a short walk, but it wasn't impossible, and in the snow, with her rubber boots on, and two pairs of socks inside, and Matt to hang on to, and at night, with all the Christmas lights sparkling—Katie wanted to walk there on this special night called Eve, and get ready for the special next day called Morn.

"Pageant's over," said Mrs. Rowen. "They do that at the eight o'clock service. It's nine now."

They had had the pageant without her?

"I missed it?" said Katie, stricken. It's my fault, she thought, I should have asked earlier. I didn't know I had to ask earlier.

She pushed the sadness away from herself, thinking, When I have a family, they'll know these things; they'll know you have to plan earlier.

Mr. Rowen said, "They have an eleven o'clock service, though."

Katie knew they would not let her go to that. She never got to stay up that late. In the dark of her room, she stayed up, staring down the hillside at the ruby red taillights of traffic, but *real* staying up, with your clothes on—no.

Anyway, Mr. and Mrs. Rowen were giving each other those tired looks, those looks that said, I can't manage that. That's too much to ask.

So Katie didn't ask.

She laced her hands together, and stared at her fingertips, and wondered what her family was doing now, and if they had gone to the pageant and wished they could have brought her.

On a cold winter's night that was so deep

·҉·

The temperature began to drop. It slid from thirty degrees to twenty. The wind picked up, and the temperature went down another six degrees. The cold was suddenly bitter.

Allison Kitchell was glad to be inside, where it was warm, and where her father had lit fires in each fireplace. Everything about Christmas was warm: the colors, the textures, the closeness.

Allison wanted nothing at all to happen for a long time, maybe for weeks: she wanted to sit inside this warmth, and have her family around her, and get peaceful all the way through, right to the dead place where her lost child lay.

Next door at the church, the first Christmas Eve service was over, and a farmer was loading the animals he had brought: two sheep, scrubbed and wearing belled collars; a spotted pony with red ribbons in its mane, and some geese full of honking complaints. Allison pictured them against the bales of hay lugged inside earlier that evening. How the little children must have loved the sheep and the pony and the geese.

Allison had never been to any service. Would church on Christmas Eve make things better or worse? she wondered. Would I be a stranger or a friend? Could I sit among those families? See those laughing toddlers and hear those crying tired babies? Could I listen to the part about Mary and Joseph and the angel, and how their baby finally arrived?

In the breathtaking living room, with its high ceilings and dazzling tree and yellow-gold fire, Allison felt the color and carols and glory of Christmas come together—but not the purpose. Deep inside Christmas, inside the branches of that tree, inside the final verse of that carol—there must be instructions! How to use Christmas. How to be Christmas.

Allison looked at the little olive-wood Nativity from Israel—primitive, faceless peg people. She looked at the painted china manger scene from Italy. Mary sat in her blue gown, confused and beautiful, as if nobody had ever told her anything.

Nobody ever told me anything either, thought Allison.

The towering spruce beside the church was hung with hundreds of tiny clear lights. They sparkled on and off like stars in the sky. Remote and blurry and unknown. A mystery, like Christmas. You could study it every year and not have the slightest idea what it meant.

And wild and sweet the words repeat
Of peace on earth, goodwill to men

✦

Matt was wrestling in his heart.

It was exhausting, fighting yourself. And you couldn't win, either. Every time he tried to explain things to Katie, he felt sick. He'd swallow the words, and they'd move around in his gut.

"I could take Katie to that eleven o'clock service," he said.

Katie drew in a breath so deep it seemed to take oxygen away from the rest of them. She held herself completely still.

"It's snowing pretty hard, Matt," said Mrs. Rowen.

He shrugged. "It's not that far. Half mile, I guess. It'll be kind of fun in the snow. It's not as if we could get lost."

Matt never used words like *fun*. He didn't have "fun."

"Well," said Mrs. Rowen, "all right."

Katie flung herself on Matt, hugging his waist with joy. Something in her broke free, and her real self poured out. She clapped, danced, chattered, giggled. She raced around, getting her jacket, pounding down the hall, grabbing mittens, tearing back, slamming her door, giving Mrs. Rowen the brush to fix her hair, jumping up and down so that it was impossible to fix her hair.

Matt could tell that the Rowens were literally counting the hours until Katie was gone.

He helped Katie with the zipper on her jacket. It was a secondhand jacket, and the color was dull. Dark red, a boy color, instead of the frothy girl colors the other third-graders were wearing this year. It had a tear in the lining. Every time she put it on, Katie had to tuck the torn part back up where it wouldn't show.

Matt was suddenly very angry with the Rowens for not mending the tear, and then he thought: How can I be angry with them? They're the ones who *did* come through for Katie; they *have* given her a home. Nobody else did. They are better than the rest of Katie's world.

I just want them to be even better than that.

He was glad to be outside, glad it was so bitterly cold, because the weather froze up his thoughts. He had to concentrate on where to put his feet, and sometimes he had to grip Katie's arm as well as her hand, to keep her from falling. Katie loved every minute of it, and she laughed delightedly.

Her laugh was like a Christmas ornament, like a ball of glass.

Matt was slightly afraid of the church. He had never been in one. What was he supposed to do once he got there? He didn't know how to behave, and he would be the only one without a clue. And there would be people there he knew: the Knight family; the other kids on the math team; the other kids in that youth group.

He was surprised that having a companion, even Katie, age eight, made it easy to do something he'd never done before. Maybe this is what family is, he thought, and then he crushed the thought like snow beneath his sneaker.

There was no family.

As they walked, they could hear the church bells going crazy. Not just chiming an hour, but singing Christmas. The bells pealed out "O Little Town of Bethlehem," "Away in a Manger," "Silent Night," "The First Noel," and "It Came upon a Midnight Clear."

Katie burbled and hopped and made snowballs and named every single object they went past ("There's a tree, Matt"; "There's a reindeer, Matt"; "There's a Santa, Matt").

Matt said nothing.

There was quite a crowd at the church. Everybody was hanging on to everybody else to get up the steep slippery granite steps. People were swaddled in scarves and mittens and boots and earmuffs and hats—and laughter.

Matt was startled. Christmas makes them that happy?

"Look how smiley they are!" whispered Katie. She squeezed his hand, which increased his guilt. Mathematically speaking, he didn't see how he could have *more* guilt.

They entered a large front hall and were swept by the "Merry Christmas!"–calling crowd through very large high heavy doors and into the church itself.

The room was white, flat white but rich, like the wish bells. From a very high ceiling hung beautiful chandeliers with flame-shaped bulbs and pear-shaped dangling crystals. At the opposite end of the church was a tiny stage with a jutted-out section, like the prow of a boat.

The room did not have chairs, like an auditorium. It had long benches with high backs, like an old-fashioned railroad station. Thick red velvet cushions ran the length

105

of each bench, and each could seat six people. The room was divided by two aisles. Matt counted what he could see of the benches and multiplied by six. They could seat five hundred. He thought a lot more people than that had shown up.

Ushers handed them programs, fat with so many verses of so many carols to be sung that night.

The very back row was full, but they found space in the second-to-last bench. He slid into the row and pulled Katie in after him. She had the aisle, and even though there were five hundred heads between them and whatever the show was, she could probably still see pretty well. He was afraid to get deeper into the church. He didn't know what would be asked of them, and he wanted to be near the exit in case it was weird or creepy.

But most of all, Matt wanted a grown-up to tell him what to do about his stupid, stupid Christmas bell for Katie.

I have to stop the lie now, because midnight is coming, and Christmas will really and truly be here, and she can't go home believing. I have to tell her. The social worker was right; Christmas is about little stuff. There's no family. There's never going to be a family.

Scarlet apples hung in the wreaths on every tall thin window, and the scent, like cider and pie, filled the church. It was a scent both kitchen-familiar and Wise Men—strange. The organ played a piece so vivid, so full of notes and rushing excitement, that it hit Matt's pulse. The pews filled. Behind them, a choir prepared to enter. Trumpeters got to their feet.

Whatever it is, thought Matt, it's here.

He felt prickly and afraid.

It was hot packed up against all those people. Katie slipped out of her jacket, carefully holding the bad side together so that nobody would see the tear in the lining. She folded the jacket and put it behind her back for a cushion.

"Katie?" said Matt. He remembered how people wrote their paragraphs in English class: they fibbed and exaggerated, got flip and silly, made it all meaningless. He must tell Katie the way the class wrote for Mrs. Wrenn— as if it didn't matter, as if nothing mattered.

But it mattered.

It mattered more than anything in the world.

And Matt did not know how to embellish. His life had been too tough. He could only say what things were.

He made himself face her, and say it harshly, so she could not go on believing. "Nobody took your Christmas bell, Katie. The bell Pollard meant was the radiocassette wish. That's the wish you're getting. Your real bell, your family bell, got torn up by accident and thrown away. It's my fault. But nobody is planning to show up in the morning and be your family."

The words hit her in the face.

Matt turned and stared forward into a sea of hats and scarves and curly hair and bald heads and ribbons on ponytails. He raised his eyes higher and saw a minister in black walk up to the boat prow. He raised his eyes higher and saw a slender gold cross, almost invisible against the tall white walls, and raised his eyes even higher, to the starry chandeliers, and this kept the tears from falling.

Oh, weary, weary is the world

✦

"I knew that," said Katie quickly.

But she had not known that.

She had counted completely on the strength of the Christmas bell. She had seen how people smiled when they picked one out. She had believed in that paper: the paper of books and libraries and truth.

Katie had believed.

The trumpets began. They were a sound Katie had never heard or dreamed of: shouting brass. All the hundreds of people came to their feet. Nobody around Katie opened the program to read the words. Everybody around her knew the songs and had been waiting all year to sing them again. Everybody around Katie was part of a family.

"Joy to the world!" they sang, and they felt joy, and they were joy.

The carol was enormous in the room: it pressed against the walls and exploded in hearts and voices.

> *Let fields and floods*
> *Rocks, hills, and plains*
> *Repeat the sounding joy,*
> *Repeat the sounding joy,*
> *Repeat, repeat the sounding joy.*

In Katie's eight-year-old heart, one thing repeated: Nobody wanted her.

She had been told that Christmas was not about important big things, but about ordinary small things, and now it was true.

She held the program, and it too was on beautiful ivory paper, and the paper was a joke now, not something to believe in. Just something that ripped.

The service had a shape: standing to sing; sitting to listen.

Katie and Matt did what everybody else did.

Everything about the church was beautiful. The whole church was white, but the colors of Christmas—banks of deep red poinsettias, a gold cross, green wreaths—gave it depth and brightness.

They stood once more, and the carol was "We Three Kings of Orient Are." This time the people did not sing the verses. *Kings* did. *Kings* walked down the aisle beside Katie. Slowly. Regally. There were three of these kings, wearing incredible robes, whose velvet filled up the floor behind them, and each king wore an astonishing crown and carried a magnificent gift in his two hands.

This is the pageant, thought Katie. It isn't a girl's name, then. It's scary, and it isn't mine.

She wanted to hang on to Matt, or climb into his lap, put her face against his, and weep. But Matt was rigid. Staring straight ahead, never looking at the three Kings. The inch between them was too far for Katie to travel.

Katie followed the verses in her program. Each deep King voice was different. The first was mellow. The second charged like an army. And the third was sad and thin and destroyed.

> Myrrh is mine; its bitter perfume
> Breathes a life of gathering gloom.
> Sorrowing, sighing, bleeding, dying,
> Sealed in the stone cold tomb.

Katie was sick with horror. Where had that come from? Did it have something to do with the Baby Jesus? She had figured the Baby Jesus just lay there in the hay and got presents. She stared at the printing in the program. *Myrrh* didn't even look like a word. And *gathering gloom*—how cruel it sounded.

The minister stood high on a platform facing the largest book Katie had ever seen. Katie bet the paper of that book was rich and beautiful. She bet you could rip it, too, like a wish bell.

She had not known there were limits to sorrow; she had not known, because she was little, that the moment would come when she could not carry sorrow anymore.

The moment had come.

Katie was done with reading and singing. "I'm going to get a drink of water," she whispered to Matt, and Matt nodded and she slipped out of the long strange pew.

At the back of the church were doors bigger than human beings needed, as if kings and gods really did come through those openings. Katie wasn't strong enough to open one of those doors by herself, but a smiling man opened it for her, and he closed it carefully so that it wouldn't bang.

She was by herself in that big front hall. Empty now, it felt haunted, with all the people on the other side.

The outside door was just as big. She had to lean on it with all her weight to get herself outside.

It was bitterly cold. Snow had piled on snow. Beneath the gentle white was crusty harsh old snow, and beneath that was the world.

My bell was thrown away. Nobody is coming for me.

She could not believe it, and yet, she had told Matt the truth: she had known.

I did know, thought Katie. I was waiting till the end of Christmas to let myself say so.

The end of Christmas.

They were singing again in the church, and she could hear it distantly, as if she had traveled miles instead of two doors. The singing was rich and beautiful, with the heavy voices of men at the bottom. The carol was a four-part family: father, mother, son, daughter.

Katie knew nothing of these things, and now she never would.

She walked away from it.

Angels bending near the earth

:

The Kitchells' big Victorian house was full of people: cousins, old friends, strangers, and sisters. There were laughter and mulled cider; there were a roast goose and a baked ham; there were sticky breads shaped like wreaths, with candy holly and cinnamon butter. There were cheeses and salads and sauces.

When the bells next door burst into peals, carol after carol, you had to raise your voice to be heard, so they raised their voices and the party got richer and fuller.

Liz said, "Aren't the bells beautiful? Let's go this year!"

The Kitchells had never done this. They kept Christmas for Santa, not God.

"Church?" said her father, and he raised his eyebrows and laughed. He patted Liz indulgently. The guests smiled kindly, as if Liz were a six-year-old and didn't understand.

And her sister, Allison, said, "I want to go too."

The sisters tilted toward each other, as if both were looking for the other side of the Christmas tree; the meaning side—but, "No," said their mother, "I have a late dessert planned. It's in the oven. Everything is perfectly timed. If you want a ceremony, or something, why

112

don't we read a poem out loud? How about 'A Child's Christmas in Wales'?"

"We don't need to read out loud," said their father. "We have a wonderful tape of that. I'll put the tape on; it'll be in the background while we talk."

Anything important in this family, thought Liz, will always be in the background.

So how did Allison and I turn out this way? Why do we ponder and wonder?

She thought of the torn bell and wondered what her father had thought of when he ripped it in half and when he ripped it in half again.

Her father pounded down the hall to find the tape. Dad had the world's heaviest feet. Liz loved the sound of her parents in this house, Mom bustling, Dad pounding. She was swamped by loving her family just as intensely as she wanted a different family altogether.

"I know!" said Daniel. "Let's build snowmen!"

"Or have a snowball war!" said somebody.

"Or make snow angels," said Allison.

The snow in the front yard was perfect, thick and damp and sticky. Daniel lay down in the snow and swung his arms and legs until he had made a six-foot-three angel. He grinned up at his wife, letting the snow fall on his face, and Allison lay down next to him, and they made angels in a row, linking their wings, letting Liz haul them up so they didn't ruin their angels, and then hopping as far as they could to lie down again, until they had made a paper chain of angels across the entire yard.

Liz wanted to tell her sister and her brother-in-law about her secret good thing: the ski trip for Azintra; but it was impossible to talk about, just as writing anything truthful for Mrs. Wrenn was impossible. If she told, she would have to admit that Dwayne did not get his sneakers, and that Katie—Katie, age eight—had been torn twice. And where were the angels for them?

***The night is darker now and the
wind blows stronger. Fails my heart,
I know not how. I can go no longer.***

⚡

She walked, and continued walking.

Katie had no destination. She had no thoughts. She was not going toward anything, and she was not going away from anything.

She was accustomed to sorrow and acquainted with grief, so a torn and unwanted bell was not a shock. It was just more than she could bear.

The wind sapped her strength, and she stumbled. The snow and the wind shrugged.

Gathering gloom, thought Katie.

Gloom wasn't what she had wanted Christmas Eve to be. She wanted Christmas to be the other song, the Midnight Clear song.

She walked in a straight line, and because it was a city, it had straight lines, the careful grid of sidewalks, and they all led away from the church. She walked past dozens of houses, and most of them shouted Christmas: a wreath on the door, a candle in the window.

She had on her old sweater and her favorite corduroy pants. She loved corduroy. It was warmer and kinder than other cloth.

She fell on a patch of ice hidden by new snow. She had no mittens, either; they were in the pockets of her torn jacket, still on the red velvet cushion next to Matt.

She did not know where she was, and it did not matter.

She did not know why she was walking, and that did not matter either.

People had shoveled their walks and driveways, and then the snowplow had come by, blockading them after all. Katie did not want to walk in the street, even though there was no traffic. She did not want to be visible. She walked on what had once been grass, people's front yards; but something about the snow made it public property; it was all one, just snow.

One yard had a snowman, and the snowman was dressed in a better jacket than Katie had ever had.

A sob wrenched her.

A block farther, and she came to the prettiest, smallest Christmas tree she had ever seen: it was in a little tub, and snow had piled to the top of the tub, like a little mountainside. The tiny tree had tiny lights, like diamond necklaces. It was no taller than Katie, and it lay beneath its snow cover, the diamonds flickering, like stars in a distant galaxy.

I could lie down, too, thought Katie. I could have a snow blanket.

She found that she did not mind.

And she knew nobody else would mind.

Next door was a house where nobody had shoveled. Nobody had walked in and out. Nobody had hung a wreath or delivered a Christmas card.

Nobody was home.

Katie could not go to a house with lights on. But she could go to a house of darkness.

She crossed unbroken snow to the front porch and sat on the bottom step, and in the silence of the night, the snow snowed down on her.

Katie had wanted Christmas to be about big things, and it wasn't.

Her heart was broken, as if she were only an ornament, made of glass, and somebody had dropped her.

Everybody had dropped her.

For a while it was terribly cold. It hurt everywhere, not just her bare fingers, but her sides and her throat and her toes.

Then it wasn't so cold, and she let the snow be a blanket; she curled up under it, and the snow snuggled around her shoulders, and Katie found rest.

And glory shone around

:+:

The organ was so beautiful, the trumpets so splendid, that Matt's chest hurt. He wished he knew these words by heart, like everybody else. It *was* sounding joy.

When the song was over and people were shifting their bodies into the pews, Matt huddled inside his jacket, keeping the words up against himself. Holding them with his body heat.

The service went on and on.

It had a beauty with which Matt was not familiar: the words and the songs and the people and the church itself; both light and shadowed, both simple and mysterious.

He spotted Jamie in the choir, music held high, eyes fastened on the organist, and it was a relief to know that Jamie had something he loved doing. Matt recognized Jed, from math team, with his family. Tack, with his family. Church was that kind of place, a place for people who already belonged.

But although Matt did not feel he belonged, he also did not feel wrong sitting here. So this was peace: your insides lying quietly, not angry with you or the world.

You can have problems, then, thought Matt, and still be at peace.

The congregation sang "Silent Night," and he knew some of the words and was even willing to try the ones he didn't. He climbed into the carol: "Silent night . . . holy night . . . all is calm . . . all is bright"—

Where's Katie?

He'd been so careful to stay clear of her pain that he had not even looked to see if she was okay. She wasn't even here! How long had she been gone?

Matt opened the program, mentally timing all that had happened, the many verses of carols, the many verses of the book called Luke.

She'd been gone fifteen, maybe twenty minutes.

Matt picked up her jacket. It was as limp and flimsy as a dishcloth. It couldn't keep a child warm.

He slid over her vacant spot, head down, not looking at any of these strangers, tried to leave invisibly. No way. The place was packed beyond standing room. People were jammed against the walls. He had to look into their faces and motion them to step aside, smiling the apologetic smile that regular people used to get their way. Finally he was through the huge doors and alone in the empty hall.

A sign pointed to bathrooms downstairs. He ran down and knocked on the door to the women's room and called, "Katie?" He even went in to check. Empty.

A drink of water had been a lie, a way to run.

He, Matt—who could run without moving, who could take his mind and vanish while social workers or teachers or especially his own mother talked to him— knew all the ways to run.

He ran back up the stairs, finding the steps strangely high, as if he had lost the strength to lift his feet.

Where has Katie gone?

The only other doors led outside.

He went out into the snow, and the size of the world horrified him.

Where would Katie fit in, in such a huge world?

But that was the problem. She did not fit in.

It was snowing harder.

The wind bit his cheeks, and it hurt to breathe in.

He could make out nearly filled prints of small feet, the only ones going away from the church. Matt ran after the little snow prints, telling himself he would find her, she wouldn't go far.

The prints went into the street, where snowplows and sand had destroyed them. It would be guesswork, trying to follow Katie.

Okay, she went home, he said to himself.

But it was not home, not when the Rowens had said: Out, kid.

Not when Katie knew for sure that no family was going to arrive beneath the tree.

So where would she go? What was her aim?

Matt knew that Katie would not have an aim.

She was just leaving the worst behind.

Without her jacket.

The city was a stranger to him. Snow deadened sound, and the engines of distant plows mumbled like drunks. Even with a coating of yellow sand, the surface was slippery and tried to yank him down. There was no visibility; he was slogging pointlessly from one blurry yard to the next.

He went around the block and was back at the church.

Maybe Katie got cold, went in again, maybe she'd be there waiting for him.

But he knew she would not be.

Church was not their club. He'd been wrong to encourage going there, as if they would actually find something.

His sneakers creaked like old doors as they flattened the plow's fat treads. When he churned uphill, the cold wind burned his lungs.

He could not face the Rowens.

He had added to their burdens: he had set Katie up. And somehow, because life was like that, the Rowens would be blamed, and things would be immensely worse.

Okay, he had not tried all the blocks around the church. He had to try all those streets. He ran down the hill and then shifted over one block to cover new territory on his way back to the church, yelling, "Katie!" and slipping twice, but running again during the fall, yanking himself out of gravity when he could not yank Katie out of her catastrophe.

His pulse hurt. It was not a throb but a knife stabbing him in the temple.

He mapped the streets in his head and ran down another parallel block. How far to go? When to turn? How much to shout?

The third time he circled, he was badly startled to find a whole bunch of people playing in the yard behind the church. People in bright winter jackets and scarves, lit by a streetlight, had made a snow fort and were tossing snowballs.

He wanted them to have cannon, not snowballs, and

then he'd shoot them for being happy and being a family.

What am I going to do? I have to ask for help. I'll have to go back in the church and get Mr. Knight. I don't know anybody else!

—and a voice said, "Matt?"

He nearly fell on a patch of ice beneath the snow, and he thought, My whole life is ice beneath snow, and he thought, Jesus, Katie, where are you? and he thought, How ridiculous that I could think for one second that Jesus knows, or cares, where Katie is.

For the family was Liz's.

That family. Whose father had torn Katie's bell, torn it again, and thrown it away.

"Matt, what's the matter?" asked Liz Kitchell.

I hate everybody, thought Matt, that's the matter.

But he could not waste time on that, not with this wind, not with this cold. "Katie, my foster sister," he said. He heard his voice, but it wasn't his: it was raw and cut. "She thought she would have a family on Christmas morning. The thing is, you put your wish on a bell, and they hang it on the restaurant tree. The social worker wouldn't let her write that she wanted a family, because Christmas is just about small things, and a family is too much to ask for, but I thought—well, I don't know what I thought. I was wrong. I filled one out for her, it said, 'Katie, age eight, wants a family,' and I hung it on the restaurant tree. She believed. She believed she would get a family."

These people of Liz's had gathered, had arranged themselves by height or color or maybe just by being a

122

family. Matt had no group. He did not know how it was done.

"Oh, no!" said Liz, shocked. She grabbed his arm. "Oh, Matt, no! There really was a Katie?"

"What Katie?" demanded a woman standing behind Liz. She shoved Liz out of the way; she took both Matt's shoulders. *What Katie are we talking about?*

Matt had no idea how to line up his thoughts, and produce them for these strangers, and end up finding Katie. "My foster sister. She's eight. We went to church because she wanted to know what a pageant is, and because I needed—I don't know—*something*—so we went—and then I had to tell Katie that she isn't getting a family. Nobody wanted her bell. Nobody wanted her."

Liz's father was not in the snow fight, but up on a wide snow-free porch, silhouetted by the yellow ceiling light. He lived in a house two or three times the size of the Rowens'. The garage was actually a barn. They had more than one car. They probably had more than one of everything. "You tore it up," Matt said to Liz's father. "You didn't think Katie should dare to ask for something important. You tore Katie's bell twice. Once up and down. Once from left to right."

For a moment there were just people and snow.

Silence and shock.

Then Matt said, "She ran away. Half an hour ago. She's out here in the snow someplace. She's not wearing her coat."

123

Though the frost was cruel

"Dad?" said Allison. She did not know him; she did not want to know him. She could not be the child of this man. "Did you really tear up Katie's bell?" Katie! she thought. Oh, the irony of it; the cruelty.

Allison thought of "Good King Wenceslas," around whom the frost was cruel. It could not happen. A little girl could not get lost and frozen on Christmas Eve because of Allison's own father.

"It's true," said her sister. "We were all there at the restaurant, Allison, and Dad got mad because it was too much to ask." Liz reached into her pocket and brought out the four torn pieces of the Christmas bell.

Allison yanked off her mittens and in her bare hands took the four pieces gently and fitted them together. A slender gold thread still dangled from its hole at the top of one piece, refusing to give up its grip on the wish.

Katie, age 8, wants a family.

"It was all *I* ever asked for," cried Allison. "A family. And mine was torn too." Katie, she thought. She was sick from the name; she could imagine her father's emotion—but she could not imagine ripping the bell.

Her father defended himself. "It was the name," he said. "I couldn't stand seeing that name there." He shrugged, as if taking off a jacket; he was taking off his responsibility.

"We don't own the name," whispered Allison.

In the dark, in the snow that swirled in pocket lights of streetlamps, Allison could see only a few hundred feet. But this was a city. A large city. A little girl with a thirty-minute start could be anywhere.

And who would not run, when she found that nobody wanted her?

"Katie!" whispered Allison. Saying that precious name, even so quietly, released her. For she and Daniel did not own the name either; it belonged out there, in the world. Alive. And with a family, and wearing a coat.

She clung to gold thread, the thread of impossible coincidence, and closed her hand gently over the torn wish, and cried, "Katie!" and then again, *"Katie!"*

Fear not, then said the angel

✦

Not once in his life had Matt wanted to ask for help.

But this was not his life. It was Katie's.

He left Liz's family. They were a waste of time, they had their own arguments to settle, and he needed a grown-up.

He ran to the church, ran up the steps, burst into the room, and it was still packed with people, the service was still happening: they were still singing!

He had to barge down the aisle to where the Knights were sitting, and he hated that, moving around like a jerk when everybody else was sitting still, and now when it counted, Matt could not speak, he could only tap Mr. Knight on the shoulder.

And might, and might, and might to those Whose hearts are right

✦

Tack felt the presence of somebody in the aisle before his father did. He looked up to see Matt Morden staring mutely, desperately, at his father.

What's wrong? thought Tack, knowing it was something terrible, and feeling strangely honored that Matt had come to his family for help.

Tack was on his feet first, and then his father stood, and the three of them went out of the church together, and Tack thought: Maybe I shouldn't come along; Matt might not be able to tell Dad in front of me.

But he wanted to know what was going on, and he loved action. This had an action feel to it.

Matt wouldn't talk in the empty hall, but pulled them both out into the snow. It was lung-chilling cold, and Tack, damp from the heat of the bodies packed into the church, felt his skin frost.

Matt launched incoherently into a story about one of the wishes on the restaurant tree. Katie, age eight, wants a family.

"What?" said Mr. Knight. "I would *never* have put up a wish bell that said that! Tack, do you know anything about this?"

"No, Dad. It's bad enough when they ask for leather jackets." Tack had handled every one of the bells himself. Katie was a popular name this year. But there most certainly had not been a wish for a family. It was the kind of thing you had to catch; like the laptop-computer wish; nobody was going to get a stranger's child something bigger than they'd get their own kid.

"Whose judgment," said Mr. Knight, "was so poor that they would let a kid believe she could get a family for Christmas?"

"Me," said Matt. "It's my Katie, the one who comes into the restaurant. You know her. We're in the foster home together, and they're taking her away after Christmas, because the Rowens can't manage two kids. I knew she wouldn't really get a family, but that's what she asked for, and—"

Tack knew the expression on Matt's face. It was hard and it looked mean, but it had nothing to do with hard and mean, and everything to do with scared.

"—and so I filled out the wish bell with her real wish. For a family. And she believed it would happen."

Tack almost said, "Matt, how could you have been so stupid?" but he stopped himself.

"I had to tell her the truth," said Matt miserably. "I told her while the choir was singing. And now she's out in the snow with no home and no hope."

No home and no hope.

The cold entered Tack's soul.

He had never heard such a terrible list.

I always have home, he thought, and I always have hope.

He saw Matt more fully, saw that the season of Matt's life had always been winter.

We could give her a home, thought Tack. We have an extra bedroom.

But this was real life. You couldn't just add a kid to your family like that. They were barely managing the college costs for Tack's sister and the nursing home for Tack's grandmother. Tack's grandmother had Alzheimer's, and his mother went every day to see her mother during lunch hour. Like Mom could take on an eight-year-old.

He looked at his watch. Midnight had passed.

It was Christmas. They might find Katie. They would not find a family for Katie.

All is calm, all is bright

✦

Matt expected to be yelled at, to be told the many ways in which he had failed, but it did not happen.

Mr. Knight held him. The hug was a wraparound, and in spite of the layers of clothing between them, Matt knew warmth and most of all the grip of that hug: it crushed the awfulness of what was happening, and while the hug lasted, it was the world.

Matt stepped back, ending it.

"It's okay, Matt," said Mr. Knight. "We'll find her. She's little. She can't have gone far." He turned to leave and Matt was horrified, but he didn't know how to say *Don't leave!*—and Mr. Knight said, "I'll announce it, we'll get everybody out looking."

"You mean—in the church? But they're still having their songs," said Matt.

"It's almost over. I have to announce we'll need searchers before the service ends and people head home."

Matt didn't want him to announce it; it didn't belong in that service; only candles and carols and the magnificence of the organ belonged in that service. You couldn't interrupt that kind of thing, something bad would happen.

"It's okay, Matt," said Mr. Knight again, giving him a one-armed hug. "People like to be needed. They wouldn't forgive me if I didn't ask them to help."

What was it like to be Tack? Growing up with a real father who could say *It's okay* . . . and who believed it would be.

Because it depended on what Katie was running from. If she was running from life, they might not find her. She would let the snow hide her, and her silent night would go on forever.

Wing your flight o'er all the earth

✦

Daniel came racing out of the house. "I called 911. The police are on the way. They're calling the fire department too. We'll need all the people we can get."

Already the fire department bells had begun to clang, and the first siren was powering up into a scream.

"We have to start searching," said Liz. "I'll head north up our street. Allison, you and Daniel turn at the corner, that's west. Mom, which way will you go?"

"I'll stay here," said her mother. "I'm going to call the foster parents and double-check that the little girl didn't just go home."

This was reasonable. And yet Liz knew her mother was not trying to be reasonable; she was trying to stay away from effort or hardship. Liz looked at her father.

"There are going to be plenty of searchers," he said. "Police. Firemen. Let them do it."

Let them do it, thought Liz. "No, Dad," she said. "We had a hand in this. We have to help."

"It's very unfortunate," he said. "But we'd just be in the way. They'll know how to organize a search."

Liz turned her back on her father. Near the church, she could see Mr. Knight and Tack with Matt, and she wanted to join them, but she did not want Tack's family to know about the way Dad had torn up Katie's bell. But they must know now. Matt would have explained. And they would know that she, Liz, had not told; had given nobody a chance to make things right.

She would not have Tack for Christmas or any other day. He was her own lost wish.

She tried not to think of the wish. She thought instead of the time and the cold.

If I were Katie, I'd try to get closer to the restaurant tree, the one I believed in. So I'm going to cut across town and head for River Wind Inn.

She ran, yelling, "Katie! Katie! Where are you?"

She had been asking this for months, since the death of her baby niece: *Katie! Where are you?* And she thought now: Impossible. Katie again? How could she have come to us, to our hands, our family, our failures?

But why not? On Christmas Eve, with an impossible wish, why not come in an impossible way?

Snow slowed her down and tripped her up, and it felt as if it were her heart being slowed and tripped.

Loving mother, loving father,
Shelter thee with tender care

⟡

Two dead Katies.

There was no way, none.

Allison would not have it.

She had had no power to save her own Katie, but there were hundreds of searchers now; surely among them was the power to save this Katie.

"Katie!" screamed Allison, and went twenty more paces, and shouted, "Katie!" and the name she had refused to use all these months since her own Katie's death became beautiful again, and absolutely necessary. There had to be a Katie.

"Katie!" she shouted. "You can have our family!"

She shouted into trees and yards and garages and intersections. She shouted at traffic and wind and snow. "Katie! Where are you? It's okay! You're going to have a family!"

Daniel caught Allison's arm time after time when she went too fast for the slippery surface and didn't look down to see a step or a slope.

It seemed to Daniel that most of the Kitchell family stood on slippery slopes.

His wife and sister-in-law had been born to a couple who were good parents and who had brought up two good daughters—but those parents themselves were not good people. He had known not to say this out loud.

Now the truth sat like a great unwanted Christmas package.

He thought that the Kitchells would probably be fine grandparents, showering a child with gifts and pretty clothes.

But this Katie knew better: she had not asked for a gift or pretty clothes. *She had asked for a family.*

The grown-ups this year had left a lot to be desired. But the children! They desired so much.

He thought of Katie, the tiny collapsed Katie he had held in his arms only for burial.

He thought of a child named Katie, alone in the dark and the bitter cold. A child who believed she could get a family for Christmas.

Please let it be us, thought Daniel, and the thought shivered within him, and he realized it was not a thought; it was a prayer; and he must send it.

God, he said in his heart, let us be Katie's family.

"It's meant, Daniel," his wife said to him.

He smiled without smiling, his eyes searching the snow that he illuminated with his flashlight, looking for fresh small footsteps.

"It must be meant," said Allison. "We're in the right place, she has the right name, we have the bedroom waiting!"

He said nothing.

"Daniel?" She sounded afraid, as if he might prove out like her parents—a person who did not care.

"I don't believe things are meant, Allison. If they were meant—then our Katie was meant to die. I can't believe that; that our baby was conceived in love, and carried in love, and born in love—but meant to die. No. Things are not meant."

They stared at each other, struggling through the snow, struggling with their hopes.

Daniel said, "But I do want Katie. This Katie. Eight-year-old Katie. Our family took her bell, and our family is going to give her her Christmas present."

Look down from the sky

✦

Liz saw tracks cross a yard. At first she thought it was skis: a pair of ruts. But when she looked closely, she saw how the boots had dragged along, not making separate prints, but little trenches.

Liz was running now, running over a yard that seemed way too big, around bushes that seemed way too dark, racing forward, brushing the snow away, crying, "Yes, yes, yes!"

It can't be her, she thought, and then she thought, *Please God, let it be her. Let it be Katie!*

It was Katie.

Liz did not know her, but she had always known her. She knew this face, this skin so cold, this hair soaked with snow.

Thank you, God, she said, without speaking, without words. *Thank you for letting me do something good in the world.*

She had done one good thing. She had not gone back inside. She had not shut the door. She had not shrugged. She had joined the search.

"Be alive," she said to the little girl, scooping her up. And Katie was alive.

"Keep breathing," she said to Katie, unzipping her own coat and tucking Katie inside. She stumbled toward the street. Eight years old was too big to carry. Liz could only drag Katie.

She flagged down the next car, sure that people in cars at this hour were searchers themselves.

But the car was just some man arriving really late at his family's Christmas Eve celebration. Liz started to explain, tried to give all the background of this lost and frozen child, but the guy touched Katie's icy cheek and said, "Forget it, just get in, I know where the hospital is."

The crews hadn't been able to sand fast enough to keep up with the snowfall. Liz's driver careened down the road, much too fast for the slick surface. The guy flicked his brights at police cars and a fire truck and rolled down his window as he passed them, yelling, "I got her!" He was happy, this man; he was incredibly, totally happy that on Christmas Day in the morning, he got to save a life.

Me too, thought Liz.

Sing praises, all you within this place

✦

"Thank you," Matt said to Liz.

"It'll be okay," she told him, and she held his hands in hers.

For a moment, they were love.

Not *in* love. But love itself.

It was bright, and wonderful.

Then it ended. They were just people who knew each other.

Mr. and Mrs. Rowen were brought in a police car. They were weeping. "It's our fault," said Mrs. Rowen, choking with horror. "It's our fault because we told her we couldn't keep her."

"It's our fault," said Liz, "because we tore her bell."

"It's my fault," said Matt, "because I told her such a lie."

Allison said, "It's nobody's fault. It's a gift." She was laughing and crying. "Katie needs a family," said Allison. "We need a daughter."

Liz was stunned by her sister's beauty. By her belief. By Daniel, more calm and more careful, but there, just as Allison had always said: a man who would be a good father.

"I believe things are meant," Allison told everybody. "We were meant to be Katie's Christmas bell."

Matt did not believe things were *meant*. Life had been

139

too hard on Katie. A joyful, bell-ringing, Christmas Eve kind of God would have *meant* to do things quicker, and easier, and nicer.

So it wasn't *meant*.

But it was happening. The right thing was happening because the wrong things had happened.

It reminded Matt of the church itself: shadow and light. Both clear and mysterious.

There is no Santa, he thought, but—is there a God?

And all the bells on earth shall ring

✦

Tack's father was stunned and silenced by Allison and Daniel.

I can do restaurant wishes, he thought. Little steps, little stages, then it's over, nicely shaped like a calendar or a tree. But a child? A child they have not even seen? A child to whom God knows what has happened in her eight years?

Yes, he thought. *God knows.* And God knows that for Daniel and for Allison none of that matters.

He looked at his son and saw that Tack was envious: Daniel and Allison got to do the right thing. His son wanted to be the hero. Well, I've done something right, thought Tack's father. My child has a heart big enough.

He listened to Allison, and studied her face, and he, too, believed: she would be a good mother to this eight-year-old who wanted a family.

But behind her, he could see the invisible roll call of social workers and forms and permissions and interviews, of administrators and foster systems and paperwork. You didn't just show up at the door and claim a kid. Twentieth-century America could not work that way. So there was no guarantee here. Allison and Daniel, in love with having this child, in love with taking Katie home and giving her a family for Christmas . . . might not.

But there was hope.

"How can we help?" Tack said anxiously to his father.

His father nodded. "There are two things we can do," he said. He asked the Rowens if he could call the social worker assigned to Katie. "Not to get anybody in trouble," he assured them. "But to start the paperwork. Katie wanted a family for Christmas, and that's now; that's in a few hours."

The social worker on duty at the emergency room snorted, "You must believe in Santa Claus. Getting it done by morning is impossible. It would be impossible to get it done in six months!"

Matt agreed. He knew the speed of paperwork.

Tack's father just smiled at the social worker, smiled at his son, put an arm around Matt. "There is no Santa," he agreed, "but there are good neighbors."

He made the phone call to Pollard. He coaxed Pollard to leave his warm home—on Christmas!—at one in the morning!—when it was snowing and ten degrees out.

Matt looked around the waiting room. The stranger who had picked up Liz and Katie was gone. Matt had never said thank you to him. Matt did not even know his name.

People do want to help, he thought. He was stunned by the size of this Christmas present he had never asked for but that had been given to him anyway.

He watched Allison and Daniel, imagining them as parents, and he was satisfied that they would not be like Liz's dad and mom; they would be like—

—like the Knights. Katie would have a family like Tack's.

If Pollard let it happen . . . If the rules let Pollard let it happen . . .

"Dad?" said Tack. "What was the second thing? You said there were two things we could do."

Mr. Knight nodded. He walked the two boys out of the hospital, away from the doors, away from the waiting wheelchairs, away from the lights and fences. They went down the sidewalk, away from the buildings and the cars. They walked to the corner, where the wind gathered the snow and hurled it, and the sky was invisible past the city lights and the falling snow.

Mr. Knight said, "God. This is the inn. There's room. Let Katie stay."

Fast away the old year passes

Yet in thy dark streets shineth
The everlasting light

✦

Matt was astonished to be in the Kitchells' house—this house with so much room, and so little heart—for the second real Christmas of his life.

Mr. and Mrs. Kitchell were excellent hosts, and the food was wonderful and the rooms beautiful. But for Matt, Mr. Kitchell would always be a man who had torn a Christmas wish twice.

Matt stood high on the stairs, safe from the gathering guests, and the lighthearted chatter, and the flashes of cameras, and watched the rest have a party.

The Rowens wandered, awestruck by the Christmas trees. Tall and thin for the upstairs hall was a tree done only in lace and silver. Short and plump for the tabletop in the dining room was a tree covered with stars in gold and silver; on the cold and glittery glassed-in porch stood a real tree, roots wrapped in burlap, branches delicately twined with the smallest twinkling lights Matt had ever seen. And in the living room stood an immense tree, so covered with balls and swags and ornaments that its beautiful branches hardly showed. Mr. and Mrs. Rowen held their cups of punch uncomfortably, wondering when the evening would end.

On a soft crimson sofa sat the new family: Katie; her father, Daniel; her mother, Allison; and her aunt, Liz, squished together, cuddling.

Matt had gone with them to the pageant in the church next door, and they were a whole pew of beginners, new to the pageant thing. Katie loved the parade of kings and shepherds and sheep. She liked sitting on the pew between her parents, and she liked getting tired of sitting between them, and sitting on her father's lap instead. Katie had come to the other side of hope: she didn't need hope; she possessed her family.

Last year, the pageant had not taken place on a stage. There were no costumes. There was no music. But the roles were filled. Liz and Tack and Matt had been swept by the calendar as once three kings were swept by the stars toward Bethlehem. And Katie on the hillside had waited for angels, and Allison had gone to the town of her birth.

And I, thought Matt, who was I? Was I a shepherd? A wise man?

The Rowens, more than ready to leave, were waving to him. He nodded silently and headed down the stairs; stairs that were a work of Christmas art, twined with holly.

Christmas was only a chance: you could take the chance, or you could ignore it. You could offer your heart, or just deck the halls with boughs of holly.

Katie scrambled off the couch and ran to hug Matt good-bye. She was wearing a green velvet dress, with a hundred tiny buttons down the front, like a child from another century, and her hair had been curled and caught back with a shimmering ribbon.

The eyes of her family followed her.

She twirled joyfully, showing off. "Merry Christmas, Matt."

It wasn't the dress she wanted him to admire, but her place in a family who adored her.

"You look beautiful," he said.

She lifted her arms to be held. "I heard you were a star at the math meet."

A star.

Not a shepherd, not a wise man, but a star.

He laughed suddenly, and swept Katie up, and swung her in the air, and the weight of her was perfect. He had never done anything quite so wonderful as lift up somebody he loved.

"Merry Christmas, Katie," he said, and the words caught in his throat, and he had to say them a second time.

Merry Christmas.

CAROLS

Sharon Creech
Walk Two Moons

Just over a year ago, my father plucked me up like a weed and took me and all our belongings (no, that is not true – he did not bring the chestnut tree or the willow or the maple or the hayloft or the swimming hole or any of those things which belong to me) and we drove three hundred miles straight north and stopped in front of a house in Euclid, Ohio.

There, Salamanca Hiddle begins to unravel the mystery that surrounds her world – a world from which her mother has suddenly, and without warning, disappeared.

'A powerful, emotional narrative which keeps the reader guessing right up to the end.'
Smarties Prize judges

'A really satisfying book – funny, poignant, cunning in the unravelling of its mysteries.'
Observer

Winner of the Newbery Medal
Winner of Children's Book of the Year (Longer Novels)
Shortlisted for the Smarties Book Prize
Winner of WH Smith's Mind-Boggling Books Award

Karen Cushman
Catherine, Called Birdy

Dear Diary

20th Day of March, 1291

Shaggy Beard wishes to take me to wife! What a monstrous joke. That dog assassin whose breath smells like the mouth of Hell, who makes wind like others make music, who is ugly and old!

Corpus Bones, I must make a plan. Luckily I am experienced at outwitting suitors . . .

Catherine's in trouble. Her father's trying to marry her off to disgusting old Shaggy Beard, and her mother's determined to turn her into the perfect medieval lady. Will either of them succeed? Not if Catherine has anything to do with it!

Runner-up for the Newbery Medal
Shortlisted for WH Smith's Mind-Boggling Books Award

A selected list of titles available from Macmillan and Pan Books

The prices shown below are correct at the time of going to press. However, Macmillan Publishers reserve the right to show new retail prices on covers which may differ from those previously advertised.

Caroline B. Cooney
What Child is This?   0 330 37053 7   £3.99

Karen Cushman
The Midwife's Apprentice   0 330 34961 9   £3.99
Catherine, Called Birdy   0 330 34524 9   £3.99

Sharon Creech
Absolutely Normal Chaos   0 330 32226 5   £3.99
Walk Two Moons   0 330 33000 4   £3.99
Chasing Redbird   0 330 34213 4   £3.99

Elizabeth Laird
Red Sky in the Morning   0 330 30890 4   £3.99

All Macmillan titles can be ordered at your local bookshop or are available by post from:

Book Service by Post
PO Box 29, Douglas, Isle of Man IM99 1BQ

Credit cards accepted. For details:
Telephone: 01624 675137
Fax: 01624 670923
E-mail: bookshop@enterprise.net

Free postage and packing in the UK.
Overseas customers: add £1 per book (paperback)
and £3 per book (hardback).